BENEATH THE MANTLE

AHIMSA KERP

Severed Press
Hobart Tasmania

Beneath The Mantle

www.severedpress.com

ISBN: 978-1-925225-83-9

Chapter 1

He couldn't stop smiling. "Look! I found penguins," Stuart said. He raised his camera and zoomed in, holding his camera as still as possible, and wishing he had brought one of his tripods with him. These were the first penguins he had ever seen outside of a zoo. "They dressed up for us too," he added. "Put on tuxes and everything."

"Nice camera," a soft voice said beside him. Keshav, the English chap who was there with his wife on their honeymoon, stood beside him. Keshav wore his saffron orange turban, a warm beard covered his face, and a point and shoot dangled on his chest. He reached for Stuart's Sony. "Mind if I take a look?"

Stuart hesitated. "Actually, it's a very expensive camera," he explained. "I'm more comfortable keeping it in my own hands."

Keshav laughed. "Fair enough, mate." He raised his own camera and began to snap photos.

With the low resolution of a point-and-shoot, Stuart wasn't sure why he bothered. There were much better photos on the internet already.

The penguins sat on something like a small frozen island or the tip of an iceberg. There were three of them, and while they didn't do anything interesting, two slept, and the third groomed himself under his armpit, they were indisputably real wildlife. It made the high cost of this cruise already seem more reasonable.

"Do you know what kind of penguins these are?" Keshav asked while he took blurry photos without regard for aperture or framing.

Stuart had to resist the impulse to lecture him on the merits of mirrorless. He reminded himself that not everyone was here to blog or on a six-month trip around the world.

"They're Gentoo, I think," Stuart said. "I've been researching for my blog."

"They're Adelie penguins," interrupted a voice. They were joined by Harper Gomez, the paleontologist who had been to Antarctica before. "You can tell from the white ring around their eyes."

Keshav nodded. "Thank you, Doctor Gomez." Keshav Sing was a tall, well-mannered man. His accent sounded of the Midlands, not the Punjab.

"Ah, I wasn't quite sure," Stuart said to the doctor.

She ignored him. Had been since two nights ago.

"And where's Baruna?" she asked.

Keshav waggled his head ever-so-slightly. "She's feeling a bit ill. Never been on a ship before, and although the *Pantheon* is quite large, she can still feel the sea."

This bored him, and Stuart stopped listening as he snapped more photos. Not many bloggers had been to Antarctica, and he could really break into the business this way. He started to write the post in his head. *Today I saw* ... Shit. What was a group of penguins called? A colony? A pack? A pride? Something he'd have to check back in his room, if the Wi-Fi actually worked yet. It hadn't so far, which annoyed the piss out of him, because he had paid quite a lot of money to join this cruise.

Keshav said goodbye; he had to check in on poor seasick Baruna. He left, and only Harper and Stuart remained along the rail by the grey sea. It was his chance.

"Harper?" he said. His voice sounded more tentative than he intended. "I mean, Doctor Gomez, if you'd prefer."

She already had walked away. But she stopped, turned around to face him. Her nose was too big for her face, and her light brown hair badly needed highlights. Stuart refrained from telling her that though. People didn't appreciate good advice. Besides, she was mostly beautiful; tall and tan and lithe. Intelligent of course: she was a doctor. Just now, however, her face had the vaguely pained expression of someone removing a splinter. "To be quite honest, I'd prefer you didn't talk to me at all."

"Listen, about what happened in Ushuaia."

"Nothing happened in Ushuaia," she instantly corrected him.

"I was too drunk and too excited. Trip of a lifetime, right? I'm sorry. It won't happen again."

She stared at him for a long moment, as if by doing so she could establish his sincerity.

"I'm sorry," he said again.

She sighed. "Fine. I'll write it off as a youthful indiscretion. You're not the first guy to kiss me when I wasn't looking, believe it or not."

Her voice trailed off, and her eyes grew wide as she stared behind Stuart, toward the sea.

"The mist," she said. "It's coming in fast."

Stuart whirled around. The penguins were gone, hidden in the depths of the fog. The place they napped, be it land or glacier, had likewise disappeared. A wind blew in, cold and biting, and they both shivered. Stuart had grown up in Winnipeg, and he knew a thing or two about winter weather, but this was something else. This was a chilling attack, a frozen challenge from the depths of Antarctica.

"The captain said we'd have sunny weather until tomorrow," Stuart said. He needed to get his hat and gloves soon.

"Welcome to the Drake Passage," Doctor Gomez said. "It's unpredictable and chaotic. Things get real weird here."

She was about to leave. "Do you want to have dinner tonight?" Stuart blurted out.

She shook her head before he had halfway finished. "I'm joining Dean tonight. Even if I wasn't, the answer would be no." There was no apology in her tone, nor was there malice or anger. She simply stated a fact.

"Oh right, alpha male is the dude for you," Stuart, hurt, blurted out.

"What is or isn't right for me is none of your business. I knew you weren't really sorry." With that, she turned and left.

Stuart, wrapped in fog, had rarely felt more alone in the world.

He stood there, for a minute or an hour or a lifetime, until he realized that a server waited before him. The man was Filipino, like so many of the staff. They could work for a few months here and make more than a year at home. There was a blog post there; or maybe a series of interviews. Or he could write the article and sell it to *Travel Jacket*, or the *Conquistador*. They loved that minority storytelling shit.

"Are you okay, sir? You're shivering."

"What? Oh yes, I'm fine. What are you doing out here?"

"Dinner is ready, sir."

3

***

Dinner was found in the form of three long buffet tables. The food was exactly what you'd expect, but it was fun to compare notes with the other passengers. He'd met some while still in Argentina, but others had joined late or not accompanied them to the bar for the meet-and-greet. Stuart showed everyone his pictures of the penguins; he'd taken thirty-four shots altogether, and not a one of them was worth deleting. The lady across the table from him thought she had seen a whale, though she hadn't had her camera at the time. And Keshav, who sat to his right, spent a good fifteen minutes telling Stuart about how he had seen a giant petrel without ever actually including what a giant petrel might be.

Baruna remained in her room, still sick, and there was no sign of Doctor Gomez or Dean Maxwell, her hairy brute of a date. But even as jealousy simmered in him, Stuart enjoyed his pasta and sushi. The crowd was lively, and people excitedly chattered. An hour of repeated visits to the buffet table had passed when Captain Kugeon strode in to make an announcement.

His smart blue jacket contrasted strongly with faded khaki cargo shorts. *The man must be crazy to wear them in this weather*, Stuart thought. He was in his forties probably, and his light brown hair and goatee made him look somewhat like Jeff Daniels. The kind of guy you knew just by looking at him that really enjoyed the Grateful Dead. With him were three other officials, including the hotel director, and the chief engineer. The engineer tapped at an iPad, frown on his face, while the other two merely hovered nervously.

"Folks," the Captain said, voice drawling. "Something ain't quite right."

Chapter 2

It's minus ten degrees outside, and the ship, big as an airport, is tossing and turning in the waves. Everyone says it's unusual, but apparently the motto here is to 'Expect the unexpected.' All I know is that I'm lucky to still be alive.

Today started beautifully. We left the town of Ushuaia early in the morning, and soon, Argentina, and land itself, was a distant memory. I can't exaggerate how beautiful it already is. The water was so blue, with stark white blocks of ice here and there. I've been to Jasper, Banff, along the Icefields Parkway and through the Canadian Rockies. This was better. More, I don't know, dramatic. It's the end of the world down here, and I feel fine! (Hmm. That might be a good blog post.)

The only problem is there was no Tim Hortons. The coffee here is about as good, but I sure do miss those donuts. My mouth is watering right now just thinking about it. They told us our phones might not work. I called my brother James for about two minutes today, but kept trying after that and got absolutely nothing. Wi-Fi has been non-existent so far too, which is really annoying. I complained twice, but they just made fun of me, smirking behind their uniforms. We paid for it though. We should at least get a discount. So far the Pantheon has little to recommend for it.

I spent the morning swimming in the pool, and then a few hours in the sauna. They cleaned my room and moved my cameras without asking me. That pissed me off, but I didn't say anything. But, Jesus, they could have dropped them or scratched the lenses or stolen the memory cards. I was in a bad mood for a while, but then things got better. This afternoon I saw penguins. Gentoo or Adelie, no one was sure. We should see Emperors soon, I'm sure. And then the fog rolled in. It was beautiful, mysterious and forbidding, and cloaked us all in a soft cushion.

But something was wrong. At dinner, the captain came in and made a big announcement. The weather has changed for the worst, and the wind won't stop. It's howling with the voice of a thousand wolves, and even down here in my little cabin, I can still hear it. The long and short of it is that we can't take the Drake Passage.

It's too dangerous. Ships do wreck here, and although there was some complaining, I think they made the right call. I assumed we'd head back to land, but instead, the Captain is taking us a different way. I'm not sure if he said "Beatle," or "Beagle," but either way, that's where we're going. If that doesn't work, it's back to dry land and a partial refund. It better work.

I feel a bit like Frodo when Sauron kicked them off Caradhras. Now we're delving into the Mines of Moria, exploring the unknown. What balrogs shall we awake, I wonder? But I didn't even get to the best part. Right after the Captain made his speech, the whole ship vibrated. And then we started tipping. We'd hit an iceberg! Just a little one, and we crushed it, but still. The tables went flying, and there were broken wine glasses and plates and food; a huge mess everywhere. With all that broken glass and the ship turning like that, something dangerous literally could have happened right then.

I went to bed early tonight. No one is my age. They're all old, except one lady, a biologist or paleontologist who has worked on these ships before, explaining wildlife to all us tourists. I don't think she likes me. Anyway, the ship is rocking, and the winds are blowing. I'll upload this, and some great penguin photos, just as soon as we get Wi-Fi.

Chapter 3

Baruna felt better and had joined Stuart and Keshav in a large banquet hall filled with an impromptu buffet table of fruit, croissants, and pancakes. The primary dining room was still closed, but this room felt more cozy anyhow, though that might have been because it felt more full even with only some twenty people inside.

It was cold, and all of them wore down jackets. Stuart sipped decent coffee in a brightly colored plastic cup as he fought to warm up. They were seated in chairs that were fuzzily orange or green and seductively hard to get up from. The insistent fog blocked the windows on either side, and in front, was the bridge, where several officers studied instruments and charts. The ship had bobbed in the heavy water all night and from the bleary eyes and sluggish movements of his fellow passengers. Stuart judged no one had slept well.

He'd had strange dreams. He took an algebra test at high school, everything normal, except his teacher was a Stegosaurus. The last question on the test was simply: Why did we go extinct? Where did we go wrong?

He still heard the dinosaur in his mind's ear: *Where did we go wrong?*

Keshav and Baruna spoke amongst themselves, but now Keshav turned to Stuart.

He gestured at Stuart's camera. "How can you take photos with all this fog around?"

"My camera is weatherproof," Stuart told him. "It's why I picked Sony. I also have a waterproof case for it, and I seal it in a plastic bag."

"You don't take any chances," Keshav said.

"Indeed," said Baruna. "You can take a great many pictures of white clouds." She poked fun, but gently so. Stuart liked it when chicks teased him a bit.

"Not that it matters what I take pictures of. There's still no fucking Wi-Fi," Stuart said.

"I'm not being funny, but you Americans are obsessed with Wi-Fi signals and peanut butter," Keshav said.

"First of all," Stuart said. "I'm Canadian. North American, but not American. Do you see a gun in my pocket? Therefore, it's Wi-Fi and maple syrup we're all obsessed with."

Keshav's turban shook silently as he laughed. "Fair enough, mate, but aren't you here to unwind?"

"Read a book," Baruna added. "Or do some Sudoku."

"You know, I'm a travel blogger." He had mentioned it to Keshav a few times, but Baruna represented an untapped market.

"Very nice. What is your blog called?" she asked.

"Elementary, My Dear Holmes," Stuart said. He saw their blank looks and he added. "You know, because of my last name. It's Holmes."

"Is your blog about education?" Keshav wanted to know.

"Well, no. It's an allusion. You know, Sir Arthur Conan Doyle."

Shouts from the bridge interrupted him. They all looked up at the panicked men. Something dire had happened, and the worst thing was that Stuart heard no anger in the shouted voices. He heard only fear.

He and the honeymooners walked to the front of the room to the bridge. The boat continued to sway, but either it was better than the night before, or they had all gotten used to it. The door remained open, but there wasn't room to enter. It was not a large area to begin with, and in addition to the captain, the chief engineer, the hotel director, and the deputy captain, Dr. Harper Gomez and Dean Maxwell had also crowded in. All of them pointed through a window that was nearly opaque from the fog. The engineer shouted at the hotel director, the captain shouted at the deputy captain, and everybody wore the stunned, disbelieving look of someone who has just learned very surprising, very bad news.

"Excuse me," Stuart said. An immediate silence fell over the bickering officers. Until now, they hadn't noticed him. It was hard for him to be impolite, but he pressed on. "What's going on?"

He could feel the discomfort, and he shrunk away from the sudden scrutiny. Maxwell Dean, the big fellow who'd eaten dinner with Doctor Gomez the previous night, eased his way out.

"Listen guys," Dean almost sounded Canadian, but he was in truth from a small town in Alaska, the kind of place where kids know how to ski and shoot before they can walk. "There's no need to panic."

"We are not panicking," Keshav said.

"Is there a reason to worry?" Baruna asked. Unlike her husband, she still had a faint Indian lilt in her voice.

"You want to tell us what's going on?" Stuart added.

Dean paused for a moment. His plaid shirt was red and brown, and with his orange-brown beard and wide shoulders, he looked like he'd rather be sawing down trees in a primeval forest than dealing with over-curious passengers.

"Listen, usually these big cruise ships take the Drake Passage. The weather can be bad, it's true, but it's plenty big enough to maneuver in. Normally this is dead easy. Autopilot can take us all the way there. The bridge only has a junior officer or two, to monitor things."

"But the captain said the Beagle Passage last night," Stuart said. *Where did we go wrong?*

"The other two passages, Magellan Strait and Beagle Channel, well the weather tends to be better, but they're too narrow for most modern ships. Wintertime, they do get icebound, and the wind can blow so strong that ships struggle to move at all. You're right, we are in the Beagle Passage now. Captain himself took us here in the night. Drake was the worst I've ever seen it, and I've been tagging along on these things for over three years now. It was try this or go home, and the senior staff decided we try this."

"So what is the problem?" Baruna questioned.

"Well, the problem is that the weather isn't getting any better. There's some weird electricity in the air, and instruments aren't exactly working."

"Maxwell," the captain barked from inside. "That's enough."

Maxwell Dean shook his head slowly. "I'm only telling them the truth, Captain. They deserve to know."

"Do you want to cause a panic?" Dr. Gomez asked.

"I want them to know what's happening."

"What's happening?" asked Stuart and Keshav at the exact same time.

"Our instruments stopped reading hours ago. The radio doesn't work, and the engine just shut off. We're drifting," Maxwell Dean said. "It's like technology has failed us."

"Just tell them everything, *mensa*," Doctor Gomez said to him.

It was then, while the trio digested that news, that the bobbing ship slammed into a glacier. As they caught their balance, a massive chunk of ice soared toward the front of the ship. The window was strong; of course it had been made to resist all that nature could throw at it, but nature had been made to exceed the boundaries mankind was always trying to put on it. The instrument panels were left smoking, sparking wreckage. The chief engineer and the deputy captain were crushed and instantly killed. The captain had his left arm smashed, pinned beneath the boulder.

And the front of the ship dipped down as it began to sink.

Chapter 4

Fuck. I don't even know where to start. We struck disaster today, literally. The ship hit an iceberg, or the other way around. I guess it depends on your perspective. When we hit it, not only did the front of the ship tear open, but a Volkswagen sized, rock-hard chunk of ice flew into the bridge. There were others that smashed different parts of the ship, killing or wounding those unlucky enough to be beneath them. I was right there, at the bridge, when the ice struck. I saw two men die right in front of me. It all happened so fast. Captain Kugeon is injured, bleeding internally, and the radio still won't work. Wi-Fi remains down, of course, and nobody can get their phones to work at all. We are on an island, alone. The ship is falling apart, and if the ice weren't holding us up we'd be under water right now. Where did we go wrong?

I don't know what to do. I don't know why I'm writing. If we sink, my laptop will surely be destroyed. It helps me relax though. A lot of the staff panicked today, and jumped ship. They're all dead now, or so we think. The kitchen is gone, along with much of the food. We're lucky to be alive, and it is mostly for one reason.

Dean Maxwell. I thought of him as a good-old-boy, a hick. But when shit went down today, he was like Bear Grylls out there. He got all the survivors together, moved us to the safest part of the ship, and set us to doing small things so that we didn't freak out too much. I helped bandage people with cuts. Who knew that first aid course would come in handy so soon, eh? Thanks mom.

It's so unreal. It feels like a bad dream. I think we're all wondering when we might wake up. Like I said, the ship is barely afloat. Maxwell, Doctor Harper, and some others are leaving tomorrow morning. Apparently there are some small islands, the Diego Ramirez islands, about twenty kilometers from here. They're going with a group of five and I volunteered. My skiing skills convinced them. I'm not sure why they chose the Indian honeymooners, unless it was pity. Surely Maxwell knows that the only chance at survival is leaving the ship. We should probably have everybody leave, but who knows how strong the ice is? Some people are determined to wait for a rescue. The cruel irony is that we're not that far from land! If this fog would lift, they'd find us immediately. And Robert Falcon Scott died, what, eleven miles from his camp?

I've got to try and get some sleep before tomorrow. We're setting out at dawn. I'm scared, but it's better than sitting here, waiting to die. And besides, it will make for a good blog. If I survive.

Chapter 5

In the early morning, as an icy wind blew in from the south, amidst sheets of blue-grey ice and chunks of rock and glacier looming in the fog, and with a cold so bitter it knifed through clothing and skin, they met on the ice. They were bundled in puffy jackets layered over fleece layered over polyprop, and their breath hung in the air like little clouds.

They'd been lowered into a lifeboat, and once on, the ice the damage to the big cruiser was shockingly clear. The big ship had been ripped and battered, and it was indeed true that ice was the only thing that kept it afloat.

"There's really a radio on this island?" Stuart asked, to no one in particular.

"There should be," Dean Maxwell answered. He was the only one who didn't wear a big jacket; he had instead opted for a blue fleece vest that covered his flannel shirt. "I was there four months ago. I used it myself. Of course, I took a boat there last time. The sea freezing up like this is unusual, to say the least."

"Expect the unexpected out here," Dr. Gomez said. "That island is our best chance at survival."

"I'm ready," Keshav said. He and his wife looked out of place, ungainly on the ice. But Baruna was in med school, and bringing someone with healing knowledge was a sound plan.

"Baruna is almost a doctor. It makes sense. But what about him?" Stuart asked privately to Maxwell. He pointed to Keshav.

"Well," Dean Maxwell said. "Baruna is more than just a doctor. Besides, if I've learned anything in my thirty-three years, it's that you can never have too many big guys with beards on your team."

"Fine. Where are the skis?" he wondered.

"Can't ski here," Maxwell said. "The ice is far too dangerous."

"We're walking twenty kilometers?" Stuart asked. "I thought you wanted me here for my skiing prowess."

"Well it's certainly not for your charming personality," Doctor Gomez said, too loudly for it not meant to be heard.

Baruna and Keshav were huddled together, as they sought protection from the wind.

"It's not twenty kilometers," Maxwell said. "More like eighteen and a half. Need I remind you that you all volunteered?"

No one answered him.

"None of this would be necessary if we could get our phones or radio working," Maxwell added. "Technology," he said, using it like a curse word.

And thus the quintet set off, slipping on the ground, walking around boulders. If it hadn't occurred to any of them before that this was highly dangerous, it certainly did now. Wind whipped at them, cutting through their layers. The footing was always uncertain, and they had to go one at a time, testing each step. After about an hour, the mist burned off, revealing just how dramatic their surroundings were.

Stuart took several photos, falling behind the group as he unwrapped his camera from its plastic bag and waterproof case. He had to dig past his journal, an extra memory card, two spare batteries, a headlamp, and a small collapsible tripod to find his camera cord. His backpack was fuller than it should have been. In addition to the camera equipment, he had brought a flashlight, several granola bars, and a small first aid kit. It paid to be prepared.

No photographer could resist the starkly dramatic scenery; glaciers shades of blue he'd never seen, black, volcanic rocks, and a blue sky that stretched seemingly forever. Stars were dimly visible in the morning sky, but there was something strange about them.

It took longer than he realized to take the photos, and Stuart hurried to catch up with the others. He found Doctor Gomez. She looked at him coolly as she knocked ice off of her boots.

"Doctor Gomez," he said. The Indians were a few minutes ahead of them, and Dean Maxwell was so far ahead that he was already out of sight.

"It's spooky to think that the ice could break anytime," she said. "We are walking across frozen ocean right now. It's interesting how terrifying I find that prospect to be." Her voice sounded small.

"Look at the sky," Stuart said, trying to distract her. "You can still see the stars. There's something wrong with them."

"There's nothing wrong with the stars," she said. The irritation sounded plain in her voice. "We're in the southern hemisphere. They're just different here." The wind whipped at them with frigid force.

"That's not what I'm talking about," Stuart said. "I've been to New Zealand, and I've seen the Southern Cross. I mean, these are stars I've never seen before."

She looked up again. In the faint light, it was hard to see them at all. "I'm not sure," she said. "Look, we are falling behind."

They hurried to catch up, and soon the stars were too dim in the brightening sky. The sun, though, did not rise; it hung on the horizon, as though someone had pressed the pause button. It wasn't long before they caught up with the other three, who were huddled together against the chill wind. Maxwell looked unhappy. "Try to stay together," he said. "And let's not take longer than we need to. The longer we're on the ice, the more likely we die."

"Look on the bright side," Stuart said. "We're finally getting some nice weather."

But Dean shook his head. "That is the worst possible thing that could happen right now."

"Why?"

"The warmer it gets, the more likely this ice will melt and crack. We still don't understand how it froze so quickly, so early in the season. This sun could be our death sentence."

"Well, don't sugarcoat it for us," Stuart said. But no one laughed at his joke.

Three hours later the strangest thing happened. Stuart had fallen behind again; he understood the necessity of speed, but it was impossible to resist so many photos. This would make his name in blogging. Besides, it wasn't like he was getting out his tripod, like he should, for these shots. He hadn't told anyone that he had a portable tripod in his backpack. If they radioed for help from the island, he could take it out, and get some great photos.

As he dropped the camera back to its resting spot on his chest, his foot slipped on the ice. He fell but did not touch the ground. For one moment, Stuart Holmes floated in the air. It was like gravity was late to work that day. He hung there, horizontal, almost four feet in the air. And then a second or two later he landed back on his feet. Stuart jogged carefully to catch up with the others.

He couldn't tell them about it. They already thought him a callow youth. This unbelievable story would merely convince them of his growing insanity. And could he be sure that it had happened? Perhaps lack of sleep had caught up with him.

He caught up with Doctor Gomez, who had fallen behind the others again.

"Hey!" Stuart shouted again. Now she heard him and shook her head, as if clearing away the mental fog. "We have to catch up. Come on."

"I can't get up there," she said. Harper Gomez pointed to a wall of ice and snow, a two meter tall obstacle stood before them. Stuart had climbed many such places, though he regretted lack of crampons and ice axe.

Together they crested it, sliding down on their butts to get down the other side. The other three ice walkers were not in sight at all. As they stared, eyes squinting in the growing light, a loud cracking filled the air.

"Mother. Fucker," Stuart said. He grabbed Doctor Gomez's hand and pulled her forward. "Come on," he shouted. "We have to run."

The ice had begun to split. Zigzagging chasms appeared around them, and the cracking of the ice sounded almost like gunshots.

Doctor Harper had not removed her hand from Stuart's. But she wasn't panicking. "There," she said, her voice sounding as calm as though reading from a newspaper.

They darted off to the right, in the direction that she had indicated. There was no time for fear, no time for second-guesses, or even first-guesses; it was a time for action, and they sprinted across the ice.

It cracked before them, all the way through. They came to a skidding, slippery halt just before a three meter drop into the dark water below.

"It's breaking up!" Stuart said.

"Jump," Doctor Harper shouted back.

"Are you crazy?" he asked. The split already stretched almost a meter wide.

She leapt. Her long legs carried her across, and she made it over, just barely. "Come on," she said.

"Oh hell," Stuart said. He took a few steps back and then charged forward. His camera bounced uncomfortably on his chest. He didn't mean to close his eyes, but in retrospect, it might have been what saved him.

His left foot just touched the other side. With slippery momentum, it carried him across. He dragged his left foot and bent his knees, skating on his shoes. "I didn't even fall," he shouted with happiness.

Gomez stared at him unhappily. "We're not out of this yet, *mensa*."

They hurried on. The fog was returning, more quickly than naturally possible. "With no visibility, we'll fall through the first chasm we come across," Stuart said. Doctor Gomez did not reply, and he realized she had known this but elected not to state the obvious.

In a bizarre turn of weather, it began to snow. Not the soft gentle flakes of yuletide, but a howling wolfish storm of ice and sleet. Their heavy clothes protected them from the worst, but the wind cut through them as though they were nude.

A flare went up in the air, its red crackling energy bright enough to outshine even this sudden storm. It was maybe five hundred meters ahead.

They made their way forward. Twice more the ice cracked, and twice more they jumped across. It was impossible to see the footprints on the ground now as light faded and new snow coated the ground.

Stuart wondered now if this was how his life would end. He hoped they found his camera. There were some good pictures on there. Just then, they bumped into a dark shape.

It was Keshav. "Come on," he shouted, voice muffled by the wind and his thick jacket. "We've found the island."

Already? Stuart thought, but he followed Keshav. Soon they had reunited with the other two party members as well.

"Nice of you two to join us," Maxwell said. His eyes never left Harper Gomez's face. "Hurry; it's like this land is trying to kill us." The storm howled at them, a full scale blizzard on the ice.

"Oh turds," Baruna said. "Fifteen minutes ago it was sunny."

Stuart could see the dark shape before them that could be an island. All he could make out in the storm was a vague half-circle, but it was a chance at refuge.

The ice beneath them cracked.

"Run!" one or all of them must have shouted. Heedless of the slippery ground, of potential gaping holes in the ground, of the minimal visibility, they sprinted forward.

It was Maxwell who stopped first. He waved to the others, forcing them to stop. He had to shout to be heard over the wind, over their frantic heartbeats. The gunshot sound of cracking ice was all around them. Stuart could smell his own sweat.

"It's some kind of cave!" he yelled.

Stuart nodded, too winded to answer. A cave seemed improbable, but he'd take any refuge he could, even if it was in the mouth a sea serpent, or the stomach of a whale.

"I don't think we should go in there," Maxwell shouted. "I don't   like   the   look   of   it."
"We don't have any choice," Doctor Gomez shouted back.

"If we stay out here, we will die," Karuna added.

"I can push on, find the island," Maxwell said.

"In this weather? You're not immortal!" Doctor Gomez yelled. They were all standing centimeters away from each other and still needed to shout.

"Guys," Stuart said. "Um, guys?" He didn't shout, but he didn't need to. His camera was floating up, off his chest, and up to his face.

"How?" Baruna asked. "Are you doing that?"

"I have no idea," Stuart said. "I did it to myself earlier though."

"We can deal with this later," Dr. Gomez said. "First we need to get out of this storm."

The ice beneath their feet erupted as a deep chasm split the earth.

Chapter 6

Keshav leapt forward. He found purchase on the ice and turned around, falling to his belly. Instantly, he had Baruna's hand, and he helped her climb up to safety.

Doctor Gomez landed on a shelf a meter down and she climbed up to the other side.

Stuart fell back, so that he was now on the other side of the two-meter wide chasm.

Of Dean Maxwell, there was no sign, save for a distant splash into the icy dark water far below.

"Dean!" Harper Gomez screamed. There was, of course, no answer.

The crack widened again.

"Jump, Stuart!" Keshav called.

"I can't jump that far," Stuart yelled back. He was more terrified than ever before in his life. He wanted merely to cuddle into a ball, with a blanket over him, and a warm cup of tea handed to him by his mother.

Baruna led Doctor Gomez into the cave entrance.

"Hurry," Keshav said. "I will help you."

The ice stretched again, a centimeter or two.

Stuart took several steps back, and then charged forward. He'd done this recently, of course, but at the half the distance and had barely made it. Screaming, he reached the very edge of the precipice and jumped.

He had the distance, but not the height. His body slammed into the ice, half-a-meter below the top. Stuart's fingers scrabbled in the ice for purchase, but he felt himself slipping. Below him was a painful fall that ended with an icy tomb. His hand reached for a firm grip but he was falling. And then there was strong pressure on his wrists, and he was lifted up, out of the groaning chasm.

Keshav had him and helped him scramble out of the crevasse. Stuart lay on the cold ground for a few moments, panting and catching his breath. He hoped he hadn't pissed himself.

"You know, Keshav," Stuart gasped. "You're stronger than you look."

Keshav smiled. "I am a Sikh," he said simply. "But I'm no match for my wife."

Behind him, Stuart could see the cave entrance. It was shrinking, collapsing in on itself like a shadow bereft of sun.

The Canadian was immediately on his feet. "Come on!" he shouted. "Run!"

The man from the Midlands did not hesitate.

Keshav ran forward, charging into the rapidly disappearing entrance.

Stuart was just behind him.

It was no more than two meters high when they reached it. Stuart skidded in, sliding into first, while Keshav dove forward. They landed and looked behind them; the entrance was completely gone.

There was no sign of snow, of ice, of wind. No sign of the icy tomb for Dean Maxwell, no indication whatsoever of the Antarctic blizzard that had nearly claimed all their lives. Behind them, where all that should have been, was a sandstone wall, tinged red, with strange figures on it. They looked old; Egyptian old, maybe even Sumerian old. Stuart wished he had paid more attention in art history, and realized that was the first time he'd ever thought that.

They were in a round chamber. The ground was cool grey stone, but the walls were all red sandstone, littered with strange designs. The roof was high, 12 meters or more, and the air was jungle heavy with plants, with rot, with life. It was light in here, as though dim torches had been lit, but there were no evident sources of the light. It seemed to come from the walls themselves, as though the very air was infused with light.

And it was damnably hot. Baruna and Doctor Gomez were ahead of them, stripping off their warm winter clothes. The two of them glanced at the men, and Stuart could see tears in Gomez's eyes.

"No sign of Dean?" she asked.

Stuart crossed over to her, taking her hand. "He's gone. I'm sorry,"

She smiled then, through her tears.

"What's so funny?"

"You Canadians," she said. "Always apologizing for things that aren't your fault."

Stuart thought about how he had delayed the group not once but twice, and wondered if things might have gone differently if he had taken fewer photos. Those were uncomfortable thoughts though, and he shoved them deep down, where he'd never have to look at them again. Besides, those photos would make him a lot of money.

"Where are we?" Keshav asked. He took off his winter clothing too. "I'm not being funny, but it's as hot as the Punjab in here."

"It must be a volcanic chamber," Doctor Harper said. "It makes the most sense."

"Nothing about this makes any sense at all," Stuart said. "And there are hieroglyphics or cuneiform on the wall back there."

"Wall?" Baruna asked, frowning. Doctor Gomez looked back that way and for the first time they realized the truth: they were sealed in here, trapped.

"How did?" Doctor Gomez began.

"Nothing makes sense," Stuart interrupted. "And wherever we are, there are others here too. Look."

Behind them all, a narrow set of stone stairs led down into the darkness.

"Should we go down there?" Keshav asked.

"We can't stay here forever," Stuart said.

"But we don't know what's down there. Up here it's safe, at least," Doctor Gomez said. "We need time to process what happened out there."

"We're going to have to go down there sooner or later," Stuart argued. "Might as well go now, while there is light, and before we get too hungry."

"The rest of us should probably stay together," Keshav said.

"That makes sense. I will go alone," Stuart said. "I won't go far," he added, forestalling the coming objections. "Just down the stairs and a quick explore of the surrounding territory. The second I see anyone, I'll ask them for help. Or run away, if they look scary," he added. It seemed the least he could do after his delays on the ice.

"That might be the best idea," Doctor Gomez said. "If only Dean were here. He had the pistol."

"I've never shot a gun anyway," Stuart told her. "But I'll be fine." Only later did he realize, that of course, she meant that Dean would have gone to explore.

***

The stairs didn't take forever, but his knees were wobbling and his legs shaking when he finally reached the bottom. At first it had been a simple stairway, impossibly unsupported, and surrounded by darkness. Gradually there was life; insects (*big* insects), ferns growing through cracks in the stairs, strange colorful flowers and stalks with strange yellow growth on their top. It was really hot now, 35°C or more, and near one hundred percent humidity. Stuart stripped to his boxers and a smart wool t-shirt that was damp with perspiration.

"I never really thought about how those *Journey to the Center of the Earth* stories really went close to the center of the Earth," he said to himself. "Of course, it's hot as balls down here, so much closer to the Earth's core." It did not seem even a little strange to be talking to himself.

Here, at the bottom, was a sight he'd never expected to see, not in a thousand years. The sky was a soft purple; his sister Sophie would know the exact name of the shade, something like amethyst or smooth lilac, or whatever ridiculous names for colors they were using. And "sky" was the correct term. This far down, there was no indication of being in a cave at all. No sign of a roof, or walls, or stalactites and stalagmites. It was a world-sized chamber.

The stairs came to an abrupt stop in a great plain. The grass was thick and three meters tall. Dotted in the grass, arranged in nearly a perfect circle reminiscent of Stonehenge, were huge statues. Stuart wandered closer to one, pushing through the thick grass. His camera was reflexively in his hand.

The statue looked exactly like a Moai, one of the Easter Island statues. Stuart frowned and snapped half-a-dozen photos. He didn't bother taking the tripod out of his backpack, but these statues needed documentation. The mysterious Polynesian statues arranged like the mysterious Celtic statues was an entirely new discovery. This wasn't just number one blogger stuff, this was National Geographic, BBC, Al Jazeera. To have discovered this, he would be world-famous.

Such were his thoughts as he walked to the base of the statues and pulled his tripod from his backpack. It was his secondary tripod and only a meter tall when elevated. Still it would have to do; he'd left his good one on the ship.

A low roar rumbled through the plains. A primal terror filled Stuart as he realized how vulnerable he was. He gazed at the grass, comprehending that it provided perfect cover for any attacker. Was it moving? His heart beat faster, but the grass did not move again.

Stuart grabbed his camera, slipping the loop around his neck. He glanced up at the Moai. The stone looked worn and crumbly, and the nose was only three or so meters up. He could almost jump to it.

A low growl from far too close made the hair on the back of his neck rise. *And I thought that was just an expression.* Had he time to think about it, he would have died there. But his body took over. He leapt, his left foot hitting his tripod, and from there he sprang up as high as he could. His legs were muscled from years of skating and skiing, and he could feel them tighten as he jumped

And then came the hard part. His hands closed around the nose of the huge Moai. It was indeed crumbly enough that he could find purchase. His camera banged against the stone, and he winced, sliding it to his side. He slowly climbed up, inching his stomach over the edge of the nose. It protruded far enough out that, if he dug in, he could rest there.

It was not comfortable. His muscles would weaken, and he would have to drop. But not yet. For below him, on the plain he had just left, strode a nightmare.

It was an ugly brute. Tawny skin like a lion, mottled like a jackal, but big and hulking. A Mohawk that stretched from head to tail. And that snout! Ridiculously long, but broad, and with large sharp teeth poking out in all directions. The strangest thing was its feet. Instead of the massive paws you'd expect, it had sturdy hooves.

Above all, it was big. A lion as big as a bear is how Stuart described it to himself. But that was underselling it. He had grown up seeing polar bears in the Assiniboine Park Zoo. If, like a bear, it could stand up on hind legs, it could have reached them. This animal was terrestrial though. *Two legs bad, four legs good*! Stuart thought with wild relief.

It looked up at him, black eyes ringed with white fur. The expression was not one of hunger, or rage, but of interest. The same way Stuart himself presumably looked while trying to scrape the last remnants of peanut butter out of the jar.

The creature padded over to his tripod. It sniffed it, a little hesitantly.

"Do your worst!" he called down to it. "It's carbon fiber!" This was the stuff that survivalist nuts recommended wearing when the zombie apocalypse happened. It was not cheap.

The spotted monster opened its mouth, and Stuart saw for the first time how many teeth it had, how sharp they were.

It wrapped its mouth around the tripod and crunched down. The tripod splintered, severed in half by the mighty bite. The animal was not happy with the taste, and it turned and stared again at Stuart.

"My, what sharp teeth you have," Stuart said, quietly and with more than a little awe. His muscles ached now, and his fingers grew sore from holding his weight. He thought about sliding down and trying to land on the animal. There was no guarantee he could even hit it, and supposing he did, he would simply bounce off that bulk, and then be prone. Supper for the animal.

The thing sat patiently down on its haunches, watching Stuart all the while. *That motherfucking thing is just waiting for me to come down. He knows the buffet table will be refilled soon.* It was a chilling feeling.

Maybe only ten minutes had gone by. Perhaps an hour. Stuart's arm muscles were visibly trembling, and thrice he'd had to scramble back up the nose.

The monstrous creature remained watching him, armed with the jaws of a nightmare, and the patience of a saint. Suddenly, though, it looked up sharply, head jerking to the left. Its nostrils flared.

A three meter tall bird sped into the clearing. It had little wings on the side, and a huge hooked beak reminiscent of an eagle. The lion-like monster snarled and jumped up, but it was far too slow. The bird reached down with its beak and tore a huge hole into the other beast's spine.

The bear sized lion roared in pain and frustration, flashing its fangs at the bird.

The bird, in turn, stretched its neck impossibly, turning it almost ninety degrees and biting into the right shoulder of the roaring animal.

The four legged monster screamed again, and now pain was overwhelming anger. It lunged at the bird, for it was taller and broader, and unquestionably stronger.

Stuart reached for his camera and almost slipped. His body slid down the stone nose, and he had to grab on solidly. The friction bloodied his hands. *Both hands, goddammit. I need both hands.* Stuart felt nearly as frustrated as he had upon the ice.

There had never been a better time in all of his life to take a photo, and if he tried, he'd fall to almost certain death.

Chapter 7

I can't stop shaking. My laptop is still on the boat, so I am writing in my moleskin journal. Thanks Dad! I didn't think I would use it, but he insisted. When is the last time I wrote by hand? I'm sitting on the world's longest staircase, and I just need to take a break. My legs ache with every step up, and I keep looking over my shoulder, to make sure I'm not being followed.

If I were to tell you what I had just seen, you would call me a liar, or a madman. Hidden here, beneath this Antarctic cave, is a boundless jungle. The kind that dinosaurs once roamed, it would seem. Sweltering heat, huge bugs, grass as tall as two men. But there are no dinosaurs here.

At first I discovered something unheard of in human history. Easter Island statues arranged in a circle, a conflux of England and Easter Island. What does that mean? Surely this is something that will be studied for years. Lifetimes. If we ever get out of here to tell the story.

This can be huge for my career. I have become more than a travel blogger and am now an adventurer, a discoverer like Robert Bylot, or Survivorman.

But the statues are not the end of my discoveries. I was hunted, stalked, by a massive, fearsome creature. Through luck and my natural athleticism, I was able to climb one of the statues, but it simply sat and waited for me. I have no doubt I would be in the belly of that beast if another, equally terrifying creature hadn't come along. A huge bird, like an ostrich with a massive razor sharp beak, attacked the other animal.

I'm still shaking.

It's hard to write with a body that won't stay still. The bird pecked the monster apart. Tore him up and dragged his body away. I dared wait no longer, and I slid to the ground and sprinted back to the staircase.

I felt eyes on me the entire time. Even now, as I scrawl into this notebook, I keep peering down the stairs. If something came up here, I'd be toast. I've climbed up an half-an-hour or so, and I seem safe. Now what will the others say when I tell them what I have seen?

I have sat here long enough. My sweat is cooling, and I can barely remain awake. There's no rest here. I must press on and tell the others what I have seen.

Chapter 8

"I am familiar with the creatures you're describing," Doctor Gomez said. "The Andrewsarchus and a Phorusrhacids, better known as the terror bird. But you must be mistaken. Andrewsarchus has been extinct for, you know, something like forty-five million years. Terror birds for at least two-and-a-half million years. What's more, terror birds are now thought to have been vegetarian. There's no way it could kill a full sized Andrewsarchus, even if it wanted to."

"It happened," Stuart said. He'd arrived back at the top of the stairs not long ago to find them stripped down to t-shirts and short shorts. Immediately his story had spilled out. As he'd expected, his words had generated dubious enthusiasm, and outright skepticism. "Why would I lie about something like this?"

"Well then you're stoned or drunk," she said. "I am positive that no such creature still exists. Maybe you saw, I don't know, an emu or an ostrich. Otherwise, what you have said is impossible."

"I know what a terror bird is," Keshav said. "But what is the Andrewsarchus?"

"Well, I don't know what Stuart claims to have seen. And Andrewsarchus has been dead for far, far longer than humans have even existed. But it was an apex predator, the largest carnivorous mammal that ever lived. This is a creature that evolution created into a killer; far more dangerous than, say, a Tyrannosaur or Allosaurus."

"Stronger than a T-Rex?" Stuart asked, not able to hide his surprise.

"If estimates are correct," Doctor Gomez said. Her voice had taken on a professorial tone. "Andrewsarchus was eleven feet long, six feet tall, weighed over fifteen hundred kilograms. That's twice the weight of your average rhino, to put it into perspective. Its skull was over a meter long, and it had a bite more powerful than a crocodile."

Keshav whistled in appreciation.

"You should see what it did to my tripod," Stuart said.

"What? Why do you have a tripod with you?"

He avoided the question with the tried-and-true method of staring at his shoes. A few moments later, the paleontologist continued.

"It was too large, too effective a predator. It killed too many species, and thus died out itself. Eventually, Smilodon, much smaller, rose to fill its niche." Her voice had taken on a serious tone, but now she smiled. "A lot of that is conjecture, mind you. They've only found one skull and some bone fragments. The guy who found it was kind of an Indiana Jones: Roy Chapman Andrews. They named it after him, but if you were to name it based on what it deserved to be called, give it a true name." She paused, thinking. "*Interitusbestias*, something like that?"

"What does that translate to?" Baruna asked. She had been watching the exchange with a carefully neutral expression.

"The beast of death and destruction."

***

They walked down the stairs together. Stuart wanted to rest, but Baruna had pointed out that the ship was still stuck on the ice. Captain Kugeon and the others were still waiting for help. The sooner they escaped from this cave, the sooner they could try to fix those problems. And so they pressed on, heading down into the tropical cave. Stuart was so tired that he didn't feel pain or tiredness or anything but pure numbness.

Before they'd left, Stuart had shown them the pictures of the statues. He hadn't taken any of them from afar, but the ones he had temporarily quelled Doctor Gomez's skepticism. She had merely frowned, making a small "hmmm" noise. Since then, for the walk down, she had not said anything to him again. Baruna walked beside her, and they spoke quietly to one another.

Keshav questioned him about the details of his adventure over and over again. He, for one, seemed not to doubt Stuart for a second. He was especially interested in the details of the creatures.

"Terror birds, eh? They used to be bloody frightening in Runescape."

Stuart had never played that game, and told him so. "Did they kill you?"

Keshav laughed. "No, not at all mate. They were mounts for gnomes, and quite peaceful. But they looked shit scary."

"I see."

"All my mates thought I was taking the piss. But I had a phobia. Not a good way to get known when you're new to the school, to the city. Luckily my mates were geeks too. We bonded over games like that."

"Where are you from?' Stuart asked, having the vague feeling that he might already have asked back on the ship. He didn't have the poncy accent of someone from London, but that was all he could tell.

"I'm a Wulfrunian," Keshav said with a cheeky grin.

"Come again?" Stuart asked.

"Wulfrunian," the pumpkin-colored turban-wearing man said again, more slowly. "Can you guess where I'm from?"

"No idea," Stuart said. His knowledge of UK geography was limited to London, Yorkshire, and Scotland. "Bath?" he said, remembering at the last minute another famous place.

"Wolverhampton," Keshav said, a hint of disappointment in his voice.

"Not sure if I've heard of that," Stuart said.

"And you, part of the Commonwealth?" Keshav asked. He glanced behind him, as though asking for help from the ladies, but they were several steps back, out of earshot. "It's close to Birmingham. You know our footie team? The Wolves?"

Stuart frowned slightly in denial.

"You must know our music scene? *Mighty Lemon Drops*? *Babylon Zoo*?"

Stuart shook his head helplessly. He actually wanted to help the poor fellow out, but none of it was even vaguely familiar.

"Ever hear of *Cornershop*? You must have!" Keshav said, with a new breath of inspiration.

"Yeah, okay, I do know them. Nineties one-hit wonder. 'Something Something Forty-Five!' Right?"

Keshav looked hurt. "'Brimful of Asha.' But that whole album was good. It's not like they're *Chumbawumba*."

Stuart chuckled. "We had our own one-hit wonder in Winnipeg in the nineties. Remember the *Crash Test Dummies*?"

Keshav surprised him by humming deeply. Stuart joined him on the chorus. They sang nineties songs all the way down to the bottom, ending in a rousing rendition of "Smells Like Teen Spirit."

Stuart stopped. "I really don't want to go into that deep grass again," he said.

"Are you afraid of plants?" Doctor Gomez asked. The ladies had just caught up with them.

They looked amused and Stuart wondered if they were not also fans of *Nirvana*.

"And you such a lady killer too."

Stuart scowled. "I told you. There are dangerous beasts out here. I'd really rather stay on the stairs."

"Are you serious?" she asked. "After we walked all the way down here? With the wounded captain? Dying shipmates?"

"Not really, no," he admitted. There weren't any excuses he could think of, and fear of looking cowardly had inspired men far less afraid of him. They set off cautiously, disappearing into the grass.

He held out his hand to Doctor Gomez. She stared at him as though he was offering a poisonous snake. "We could easily get lost in the grass," he said to her.

Reluctantly, she grasped his sweaty palm. Her other hand reached back and found Baruna', who was in turn attached to Keshav. The honeymooners both grinned, happy as clams in this new world.

"The sky is so purple," Baruna marveled.

"It's like we've gone back to the dawn of time," Keshav said.

Moments later, they heard low thunder.

"I think it is coming from the ground," Keshav said.

"Quick, back to the stairs," Stuart said.

"We're too far," Gomez insisted. "Press on. Didn't you climb the statues last time?"

"That barely worked!" He couldn't hide the panic in his voice. "I can't do it again!"

The ground rumbled again, more deeply. Stuart could feel it in his gut. A sharp, bird like caw sounded; it was feral, terrible. Stuart turned and ran back to the stairs. His tired legs ached but fear lent speed to his efforts.

The others followed him, none of them objecting now. Long legged Doctor Gomez passed him, her graceful stride bespeaking a practiced runner.

As they reached the stairs, lungs burning and breathing hard, the ground rumbled and the birdlike roars were louder than ever.

"Look," Stuart said.

A dozen, nay a score of three meter tall birds with cruel, massive beaks ran in formation like geese on land. The "V" swerved through the grasslands. The terror birds did not seem to be hunting the humans and they rumbled off, away to the north.

The four of them stood there, in awe. It took some time before they began to breathe normally again.

Stuart turned to face Doctor Gomez. Her tanned skin was flushed from heat, or fear, or excitement, or all of them. Her eyelashes lowered as she briefly closed her eyes. When she opened them again, they were apologetic and full.

"What do you think, Doctor? Those still look like emus to you?" he asked.

"Stuart, I am sorry I did not believe you," she said. "I feel like an utter asshole."

Chapter 9

The purple light never faded. It stayed exactly the same brightness, and after a while, the idea of time itself seemed a foreign notion. None of them wore a watch, as all had come to count on their phones.

Even Stuart's camera, which did still work, wouldn't display anything other than a blinking *12:00*.

Keshav and Harper had smart phones, but they hadn't worked even on the ship, and they'd been left with the warm clothes at the top of the stairs.

The four underdressed explorers pressed on from the stairs, though all felt the fear that Stuart had first voiced. They came to the statues where Stuart had taken photos.

Doctor Gomez was flabbergasted. "Why are these here?" she asked.

"Depends on where *here* is, probably," Keshav said.

Soon after that, they found the shattered remnants of a tripod, along with dried blood on the grass. It was quickly decided that there was no need to stay in the area.

They crept, once more hand-in-hand, through the tall grass until at they last emerged from the green plains onto a small hill. It had good visibility of the surrounding area, and it was here they stopped to rest. Stuart nudged Keshav.

"I've been thinking about what you were saying," Stuart said.

"Eh?" Keshav asked. He was sweaty, his blue undershirt soaked through, and droplets of moisture ran to the ends of his beard.

"About the whole 'depends on where this is' thing," Stuart said. "What you said back at the statues."

"Right. You've got some insight?"

"Well, at first I thought this was a cave, of course. A big fucking cave, sure, with weird growth and such," Stuart said.

Harper Gomez, sitting cross-legged, was absently listening.

Baruna had her eyes closed and her head resting on the shoulder of Keshav.

"These animals that Doctor Gomez told us about got me thinking though."

"Megafauna," Doctor Gomez interjected.

Stuart blinked at her.

"Call them megafauna. You know. Wooly mammoths, saber-toothed tigers, terror birds: all classified as megafauna."

"Crikey, now I'm worried about tigers with swords for teeth sneaking up on us," Keshav said. "Sorry, carry on."

"Okay, these megafauna," Stuart repeated. "The statues. The purple sky that never fucking changes color. It's not just the size of this place, it's all these things."

"What are you getting at?" Doctor Gomez asked.

"I'm just saying it's not impossible that we're in a different dimension or something."

"A different dimension?" Doctor Gomez asked. The skepticism was evident in her tone.

"Something like that. You know … 'Once you eliminate the impossible, whatever remains, no matter how improbable, must be the truth.' "

"There's another possibility," put in Baruna. Her eyes were still closed.

"Yes, *jaanu*?" Keshav asked her, using the pet term in Hindi.

"It's hotter than blazes, and we're being stalked by terrible creatures. I think we died on the ice and went to Hell together."

***

They splashed through bogs and along muddy streams. The mud splashed on bare legs as all had stripped as far as modesty would allow. The heat was oppressive, and all of them had patches of sweat on their clothes. It was almost an impossible contrast to the arctic weather of the morning. The rocks surrounding them grew thicker, in shades of green and brown. More than anywhere else in this lost world, it felt like an alien planet. Some flowers vaguely resembling daisies grew, but they were not close to the water. In fact, no life grew next to the stream.

"The rocks are serpentine," Doctor Gomez said. "They're called that because they're green and scaly. The water is toxic to plant life."

"Would it hurt us?" Keshav wondered.

"You're not a plant are you? It's perfectly safe for humans."

"How do you know so much?" Stuart asked.

"I'm a bookworm paleontologist," she answered. "The things I know are many and manifest."

She spoke with exaggerated dramatic intonations and the other three smiled. Stuart liked this playful Doctor Gomez. He remembered why he'd hit on her the first night they'd met. She was a smart, funny woman.

All of them were thirsty, and they stopped and drank deeply from the river. Dr. Gomez cautioned that they could not be sure it was safe, but each of them risked it, and none felt worse for the wear.

Around them, plants grew. They were tall, like everything here. Two to three meters. And they were beautiful. Most of their height came from long stems, but the top ended in a kind of pitcher. They were either red, or green, or a combination of both. The leaves were reddish purple, covered in intricate patterns. Their tops curved, like an upside down "J."

They grew in scattered clusters, all of them well away from the stream trickling over those hard, green rocks.

Doctor Gomez stopped. "I don't like these at all."

"Do you know what they are?" Baruna asked.

"I think so. But this is a hundred times larger than they grow in our world."

"What are they?" Keshav asked. "They're remarkable!"

"Well, they have a lot of names. In Latin, it's *Darlingtonia californica.* Colloquially, it's a California pitcher plant, a cobra plant or, my preference, a cobra lily."

"They do look like cobras," Keshav asked. "Do they spit?"

"God, I hope not. No, they're called that because the tubular leaves resemble a rearing cobra."

"Totally tubular!" Stuart said. No one smiled. "We were all thinking it," he protested."Why don't you like them, Doctor Gomez?" Keshav questioned. "They're truly beautiful."

"Oh, I like the way they look just fine. It's just that one's of this size make me very nervous. You see, in our world, these plants don't get enough nitrogen. To compensate, they eat flies and other insects."

They all showed how gross that sounded with their disgusted faces.

"A plant that eats people?" Stuart wondered. "I don't think my travel insurance covers that."

"I can't say if it does," she clarified. "They haven't done anything aggressive yet. It's possible that humans have a different chemical build; too much nitrogen, or too little. Or too much of another element. It would be fascinating to study," she trailed off and saw the three wide eyed faces staring at her. "Now, let's not stand here all day."

They traveled some more across the strange serpentine rocks and through the enormous cobra lilies. They traveled this way for some time, what felt like a couple of hours, although there was no real way to be sure. Energy waned as appetites grew, but Stuart had a few granola bars in his backpack that somewhat helped stem the hunger tide. The purple light remained the same.

Gradually the brook expanded, swelling into a creek that babbled along beside them. When it veered off to the left, so did they, reasoning that following the water would lead them somewhere. Somewhere possibly with people, or an exit out of this all-too dangerous world.

Ahead of them was the largest cobra lily of them all. The stalk was almost seven meters high, and the pitcher like bulb was easily large enough to swallow a human or two.

"I do not like the look of that," Keshav said.

"Yikes. Me either," Stuart said.

"Theoretically, the fact that none of the smaller ones attacked us, or even visibly registered our presence, indicates that this one will likewise abstain from violence," Doctor Gomez said, her tone more hopeful than authoritative.

"Theoretically," repeated Baruna.

"Well that's all we have to go on," Doctor Gomez said. "Come on." So saying, she strode toward the cobra lily.

The others exchanged a quick look, and then quickly followed after her.

Stuart caught up with her.

Baruna was right behind him, and Keshav was in the back.

The Sikh's arms were crossed, and he peeked upwards, a warning scowl on his face.

Doctor Gomez strode past the plant. It didn't stir.

Stuart passed it, heart beating quickly, and mouth dry. It didn't stir.

Baruna slipped by nervously, without ever looking up. It didn't stir.

Keshav walked slowly by, hard eyes warning the plant not try anything funny. It stirred.

He had almost caught them when the plant dipped down, its head slipping around the bearded man. It instantly and completely enveloped him, and within moments, before any of the three could even breathe, it was back in place three meters high. There was no sign of Keshav.

"Keshav! No!" Baruna screamed. She ran at the plant, her small hands clenched into fists, but Stuart grabbed her and restrained her.

"There's still room in that pitcher for another person," he told her. She stopped wriggling so much.

"His eyes," Doctor Gomez said. "That look in his eyes."

This caused Baruna to weep, but Doctor Gomez did not even notice.

Stuart realized she might be in a state of shock.

"We have to save him," Stuart said. Baruna continued to struggle and he had to hold her wrists.

"How?" Doctor Gomez asked.

"Does anyone have a knife?" Stuart asked. Neither of them said anything, and he took that to be a negative.

"How do you fight a giant plant?" he said aloud. He glanced around, at the creek, the other plants, the rocks. It occurred to him to grab a piece of serpentine and saw through the stalk, but the rocks were small, and the stem was thick. It would take several minutes, and he had every suspicion that the plant would defend itself.

"All right, I have an idea," he said, speaking quickly so that his conscious brain would not have time to discard the plan. "Follow me. Stay a couple of steps behind me. When you see my feet sticking out, grab them."

Their puzzled expressions did not stop him, and he strode forward. He stopped to pick up a few rocks, which he threw at the plant. Most missed, but one stuck in the fleshy stalk. The plant quivered, the pitcher on the top turned slowly.

"Come on, you homicidal houseplant! Try me on," he shouted.

He had reached the stalk, and it still hadn't done anything. A quick glance showed that the two women were just behind him.

He thought the plant would have already attacked him. He had to make it come down, had to try and pull Keshav out before it sucked all his nitrogen out. Nitrogen.

"Sorry ladies," Stuart said. He pulled down his boxers and peed on the plant. Urine was, after all, full of nitrogen. If he showed this plant he could provide it with the nutrients it craved, it might just come after him.

It did. The cobra lily moved so quickly that he didn't even see it coming. One second he was peeing, the next second he was encased in a sticky darkness. Sharp little hairs stabbed him in all directions, and the stench was something fouler than the grave. There was room for two humans here, but they'd be pressed together very closely. The cobra lily pressed him down, and Stuart saw a brown arm.

He grabbed it and wriggled his feet. He hoped, but wasn't sure, that they were even still sticking out of the plant. Two things happened: pressure on his ankles revealed that the women had him, were pulling him free. And Keshav's head emerged. His orange turban was askew, and he was coated in juices that seemed to be sinking into his skin, but he smiled at Stuart.

"Bloody plants. I'm beginning to regret being a lifelong vegetarian," he said to Stuart, with a wan smile. His voice was strangely muffled by the plant.

With a plonk, Stuart felt them pulled back up, out of the pitcher. The hairs were erect now, clinging to him, scraping him, and stabbing him.

"Grab my other hand!" he said to Keshav.

"That one isn't working," Keshav said. Grab this one with both of yours."

Stuart grabbed it. Another big pull, and he felt his waist emerge from the plant's hungry mouth.

It grew stickier as the cobra lily fought back. Stuart gagged on the stench of carnal rot. Another long pull, and he was free to gasp clean air. His feet remained in the air as the two women continued to pull.

"He's alive," Stuart called out. "Keep pulling."

The plant pressed down on Stuart's hands.

Keshav started screaming.

"Put my feet down," Stuart said. When they had done so, he started pulling himself. "Push on my shoulders," he said, leaning back.

They pressed on him and with slow, relentless force, they pulled Keshav slowly out.

At last his feet plopped out. They pulled him back quickly, retreating from the furious flower. It flung itself at them, like a dog on a leash, but they were far enough out of range that its rage was futile. Keshav was in bad shape. A bone of a small animal jutted out of his shoulder. His skin was mottled and slightly sizzling.

Baruna rushed to hug the beleaguered man, but Doctor Gomez stopped her.

"Get him in the stream now," she said. "Stuart too. The acid is eating through them even now."

Chapter 10

Washed and scrubbed, with a certain orange turban wrapped firmly back in place, they left the barren of cobra lilies. Keshav had a broken arm from being squeezed into the plant's stomach. His face was mottled from the plant's digestive juices, and it looked as though he'd be scarred for life. He was in high spirits though.

"I thought I was dead. And what a way to die. Like that monster in *Star Wars*, getting slowly digested for years."

"I always wondered about that," Stuart said. His body stung all over, but he'd been in briefly enough that there was no visible damage. He had taken the first aid kit out of his backpack, and Baruna had cleaned their wounds and bandaged them up. "Wouldn't you just die in a day or two? From hunger and thirst?"

"What if it somehow keeps you alive?" Keshav asked.

"But it's trying to take your nutrients. Why would it want to give you some back?"

"Are you guys seriously arguing about *Star Wars*?" Doctor Gomez said. "Besides, the Sarlaac is totally different from cobra lilies. "

"Wait," Baruna said. "Look."

They were coming out of the serpentine soil. A few small cobra lilies still clung to life, but they were small, half-a-meter tall affairs. Ahead of them, just beginning to become visible, was a tall mountain range lurking on the horizon.

Much closer than the mountains were four figures. They all looked to be humans, or at least humanoid. One was flat upon the ground, and the other three surrounded it like jackals, aiming kicks at their prone target.

"We have to help him," Keshav said.

"Are you kidding? We don't know anything about that fight," Stuart said. "You might be helping the bad guy."

"That is not the bad guy," Keshav said with some certainty.

"How do you know," Stuart asked.

"The bad guy is never one versus three," Keshav said.

"Even if that's true," Stuart said. "We don't have weapons. We are two against three, and you have a broken arm."

"Excuse me?" Doctor Gomez said.

"I'm not being sexist," Stuart said. "I just know you guys won't be good in a fight."

"That's what being sexist is," Baruna said. "And you don't know that."

"All right, you guys go punch out the three attackers."

Baruna cautiously glanced at Keshav. He shook his head *no*.

"Don't be a *pendejo*," Doctor Gomez said. "Fights are won with more than fists."

***

Stuart peered out from behind a slender fir tree. The others stood behind him.

"What do you see?" Keshav asked.

"What's the plan?" Baruna asked.

Stuart looked to Dr. Gomez helplessly.

"I have no idea," the paleontologist admitted. "But I think Keshav is right. That man could die if we don't help."

"I may have an idea," Baruna said. "Though it's not very good."

All eyes fell upon her.

"*Darlingtonia californica,*" she whispered.

The two women went to collect some they had just passed. Stuart and Keshav glanced back out at the scene unfolding before him. They were being very careful not to be seen, but so far none of the men had even glanced in their direction.

The three men had ceased kicking their helpless victim. This close, he could make out more details. Though they looked human, they were dressed strangely, in dark colors with ever-changing swirling patterns running through their clothing.

"I don't know why he sent us after this *sargiz*," the shortest of them said.

"He is worthless," the second man agreed.

"It's not on us to question the Falcon Lord," the third man said.

"Indeed," said the first man.

"Let's finish this." The second man reached for something brightly colored at his waistband.

Dr. Gomez and Baruna returned with small plants ripped from the earth. Keshav frowned in displeasure as he examined the green snakelike objects, but he made no objection. The quartet charged forward.

The three assailants drew their pistols. The shortest of them licked at his lips.

"*Sargiz.* Now you die."

Something hit him, square in the chest. The pistol-wielding man looked down in disbelief.

"What?"

His two companions were hit too. Missiles hit them in the back of the head and on their arms. One missile hit the shortest man directly in the face. The cobra lilies had been torn open, and their acid splattered on the exposed skin of the three pistol holding men.

The two who could still see aimed their pistols at the charging Upworlders. As they did so, the man on the ground grabbed the foot of the gunman. He pulled hard, and the man went down.

The smallest of the men, in swirling clothes, fell to the ground, grabbing at his face. "It's burning me!"

The third one dropped to help his companion from the ground. But the original victim was now on his knees, and he held a pistol carefully aimed at the two attackers. "Drop your weapons. And get out of here."

Stumbling, cursing, the two men helped their companion up, and they fled just as the four companions reached the man on his knees.

***

The native man rose and stared at them. He was almost two meters tall and very slender. "Thank you for saving my life. I am in your debt." He stared at them more closely. "Your clothes are so strange. You are from the upper world?" His accent was stilted, overly formal, but his English was perfectly intelligible.

They nodded. The man was dark-skinned, wearing clothing that rippled as the wind blew on it. A thousand stars twinkled in the fabric of his long shirt, which went from shoulders to knees. His hair was short and coarse, and his nose broad, wide.

"It's been sometime since we had visitors from the crust," he said. "They must have left here before any of you were born. The fashions then were much more, er, conservative." He gestured to their t-shirts and underwear; which for the men was still wet from the river washing. Only now did it strike them that this would look strange.

"How is it that we understand you?" Keshav asked.

"There is but one tongue in the center of the Earth. All organic life-forms have the intrinsic ability to speak it. The gods made it so."

"Then there is a way out?" Doctor Gomez asked, refusing to get sidetracked on a linguistic journey.

"Well, there was."

"Was?"

"There is a disc of great power. The sun disc. It can be used to send your people back to the upper Earth, among many other things."

"I'm sensing a *but* coming," Keshav said, his head waggling slightly.

"It's actually a *however*," the tall slender man corrected. "However, that disc is currently owned by my enemies. They are using it to annihilate our city."

"So there *are* cities here," Doctor Gomez murmured.

"Indeed," said the victim. "Each of them older and grander than any of your crust cities."

"Annihilate? That's terrible," Baruna said.

"It is," the man agreed. "We already have plans to try and steal the disc. You have shown your mettle here; perhaps you would join us. As a reward for your efforts, I can send you home."

The four of them exchanged a glance. They had no reason to trust this guy, but he was currently their best and only option.

Doctor Gomez stepped forward. "What do you need from us?"

"Come, back to my home. Come with me to the magnificent city of Selvage."

His name was Acan; he told them this as they followed him. Acan had collected the pistols from the ground and placed them *somewhere* in his clothes, though no pockets were visible. He told them too of the xenophobic city-states that littered this land.

Powerful cities nestled comfortably in valleys, or perched high in the mountains. This land was big, to hear Acan tell of it; they hadn't seen but one corner of one district of one small area.

Selvage was among the greatest of cities, Acan said. It had been at war for over a hundred years with its rival Omphalos, the greatest of cities. Acan did not reveal the exact source of the conflict, but it sounded like a classic struggle over territory. There were mentions of betrayals, bloody battles, laser pistols, and *peace* that never achieved what they promised.

"There are fragments of our society all over the crust," Acan said. "We have been known by many names, most of them divine, but the name most people would identify us with is the people of Mu."

"Divine?" Doctor Gomez asked. In the same instant:

"Mu?" Stuart asked.

"Crackpot hidden continent theory, like Atlantis. Debunked in the nineteenth century," Doctor Gomez said.

"Do not be so quick to judge," Acan said.

They left the serpentine rocks at last and entered a pine forest. Apart from the trees' great height, it was the most normal place they'd been all day. Assuming it still was day, of course.

"Mu was home to all the gods of your history and mythology. It was highly advanced, highly spiritual. Sometimes also called Lemuria; it is the homeland of all humanity."

"Why don't you go back up the crust?" Stuart wondered.

"Of course, we can return to our old home," said Acan. "But none will. Something has changed up there, and now when we return we find ourselves unable to dream."

"That's twice you've mentioned gods. Did they live there, amongst the men?" Baruna asked.

Acan shook his head. "Gods. Men. The distinction is meaningless when you discuss beings of great power."

"You're a god?" Stuart asked. This skinny guy looked more like he belonged on Skid Row than Mt. Olympus.

"I was known to the Mayans as a god of fermented beverages. Acan, my personal favorite of many names that have been assigned to me, means belch or burp. I am a lowly deity, and always have been. But god, I am."

"Ah, a god of wine," Stuart said.

"Indeed no," Acan said. "Grapes came over with the Europeans, and they destroyed my followers. I am the god of *babringlche*, of *balche*."

"What's that?"

"Perhaps you'd call it a mead, made with hallucinogenic honey. My specialty was made from fermented honey, to which the bark of the *balche* tree has been added."

"Damn. The Mayans were hardcore."

"Indeed. Many went so far as to inject my beverages up their arses rather than down their throats."

"The more things change, the more they stay the same," Doctor Gomez mused.

"My draughts have inherent healing properties."

"It can heal the sick?" Baruna asked.

"Indeed."

Baruna and Keshav locked eyes.

"Do you happen have some right now?" Baruna asked. "Keshav was hurt badly."

"Though he's taking it awfully well," Stuart said.

"Well," Keshav said. "I hate to cause a fuss."

A slow smile spread across Acan's face. "I should have known. It is hard for me to read humans. Of course I can help. Come here. Please, come here."

He cupped his hands, and they filled with a sparkling amber liquid.

Keshav stepped up and drank deeply from the man's palm. A glowing light suffused his body, and he smiled broadly. His hand shifted, stretching back to normal. The acid holes in his face began to scab over and heal.

"Thank you," he breathed with the deepest sincerity. He looked better than better; he looked like a new man.

"Do you have more of this? What did you call it?" Stuart questioned.

Doctor Gomez caught on. "We can bring this back for Captain Kugeon."

Acan smiled. "I have some quantity of *balche* in Selvage, already stored. I would be happy to give you some."

"It is most convenient having a god on one's side," Baruna said. She rubbed Keshav's formerly broken arm, her face a marvel of wonder.

"I can heal, but I should warn that I am not a warrior, and my help is not much against the Falcon Lord. Not unless you want the peaceful, buzzing dreams I can offer. But I can summon my brother Ek Chuaj." He closed his eyes and began chanting softly.

"Ek Chuaj," Doctor Harper breathed. "The Black War Chief."

"Black War Chief?" Stuart repeated.

"What do you know of him?" Baruna asked.

"Not much," Doctor Harper admitted. "I'm not sure there is much known at all. He was the Mayan god of warriors and merchants. He's known as the patron deity of travelers, gallivanters, nomads, those who are just or seek justice. His enemies are Buluk Chabtan, Odin, Huitzilopochtli, and Ares; brutish or petty gods of war, in other words."

While she spoke, Acan was busy. He found a large stone boulder, twice as big as a grown man's chest, and picking it up with no apparent effort, he moved it to the middle of the path. He did this twice more; disappearing into the forest and emerging with heavy stone boulders. When the third boulder was placed high upon the others, Acan placed a bit of plant on the top and muttered something.

There was a shimmering haze. When it cleared, a man stood there. His entire skin was striped black and white, his mouth was encircled by a red-brown border, and a large scorpion's tail stretched from behind him. He carried a spear in his left hand and had a red woolen sack over his right shoulder. He smelled overwhelmingly of chocolate.

Acan moved with the grace of a leaf dancing upon a pond. He stood before the recently manifested god and bowed.

"Brother. So good of you to join me."

"You called. I answered," Ek Chuaj said, his voice gruff as grinding boulders.

"I did. You did. Your help is necessary to confront our opponent. It may be some fight."

Now a smile cracked that craggy visage. "I live to fight. Which of my enemies do you face? Buluk Chabtan?"

Acan hesitated. "No, no enemy so prosaic as that. We strive against a most mighty foe."

"Who is it? Hachiman? He is a worthy enemy."

"No brother, though your duels with Hachiman are legendary, and it makes me smile to remember them. No, your opponent this time is your greatest challenge, your greatest achievement."

The smile was gone. Extinct. "Just tell me," Ek Chuaj said.

"The Falcon Lord, the master of the midsun, he of the two horizons."

Acan had not finished before Ek Chuaj disappeared. One moment he was there, and the next he was gone. Like he had been ctrl-z'd, Stuart thought in a weird moment. He noticed that Doctor Gomez had suddenly gone very pale.

"I was afraid of that," Acan said dejectedly. He sat down, his face buried in his hands. "Oh, I'm so useless."

"What the hell?" Stuart said. "Where did he go?"

Acan, wrapped up in his own failures, his own grief, did not answer.

"I don't blame him," Dr. Gomez said.

"Why? What do you mean?"

"Stuart, we know about the Falcon Lord in our world too."

"I've never heard of him," he said deficiently. "Some bird guy?"

"Who is our enemy?" Keshav asked.

Doctor Harper paused. She licked at her upper lip nervously. Her eyes shifted to Acan, but his face remained forlornly buried in his hands.

"The Ancient Egyptians had a name for him. They called him Ra."

Chapter 11

After the incredible things I have seen, this journal is starting to feel a little outlandish. Who would believe what I have to say? And why do I need them to? But it's best to finish what you start, right?

Where do I start? Well we've discovered some amazing things. Some terrifying things too. Huge plants that eat people. One attacked us, and we were lucky to all emerge alive. More importantly, we've met people! Well, "people" might not be the right word. They're known in our worlds as gods. I haven't worked out if all the gods we know are down here, but some of them are for certain.

Apparently the gods have been on our part of the planet. (They call it the crust.) They claim responsibility for the pyramids, Stonehenge, Maccu Pichu and especially the Easter Island statues, which they say represent each of them.

I say "they," but we've really only met one of them. Acan, is his name. The Mayan god of burping. Heh. Alcohol too, I guess. He and his brother speak English. When we asked Acan about this, he said something like, "We invented it. Why shouldn't we know it?" It seems gods kind of innately can speak any language ever known. He has other powers, too. He can create healing draughts with his bare hands.

We actually saved him from some enemies. Apparently, he was out riding a favorite animal and he got ambushed by some rivals. They wounded and drove his beast away, but we saved him before they could kill him. Now he says he can help us get home. That is, if we can help him get a disc of great power from his rival, an Egyptian god named Ra.

I mean, I saw Stargate, but I don't really know who this Ra guy is. Doctor Gomez took it seriously though, and even the Hindus were impressed. Not that he is Ra, as they explained, but he's the guy that the Ra legends are based on. A creature of great power, by all accounts, and I'm guessing not a particularly nice guy.

All right, the lunch break is almost over. Acan found some wild fruit kind of like pears, and we stopped and ate a few while resting our blistered feet. We should be in Selvage soon, though

I'm not sure if that means in less than an hour or half a day. But I'll just finish up here while the others wash up in the stream.

Last thing. This island of Mu was apparently a super continent. Places like Samoa, Easter Island, Tahiti, even Hawaii are meant to be the last remnants of a land called Lemuria, which is just another (better) name for Mu. I don't know, it all sounds kind of, you know, chem trail, and Doctor Gomez agrees with me. She says it was a big pet theory in 19th century, but no one reputable believes it now. Keshav, who surprisingly is a bit of a geek, knows a bit too. According to one story, it was some lord of volcanoes that destroyed it. Apparently, Plato wrote about it and thought earthquakes were what finished off Lemuria. I asked Acan, but he dodged the question. It left me wondering one thing.

If Lemuria was truly an island of gods, who was strong enough to destroy it?

Chapter 12

The city of Selvage was even grander than they had imagined. To begin with, its location was beautiful; nestled in a valley between two narrow, rocky mountain ranges. A small river tumbled down from the mountains and through the valley. Fluffy fields of white flowers stretched across the horizon, and scattered copses of pines and maples, all under the purple sky, gave it the most stunning backdrop possible.

It wasn't a city like any of them had seen before. There were no streets, nothing concrete, stone, or brick. Instead there were trees, specially grown, and shaped into small buildings. Most were low to the ground, a cave made of wood, ever blossoming with leaves and flowers. Around each tree home were four curved cylinders, somewhat like ivory, but it shone like metal. The cylinders were set equidistant around the tree-homes, and each home had its set of curved pillars. In the center of the endless plain was an enormous green plant building, twenty meters high, with dark windows carved throughout the verdant monolith.

There was plenty of space all along the mountainside, and there were possibly thousands of the cave-like tree-homes.

A thought occurred to Stuart as they traveled over the last bit of field before reaching the first of the structures. "All those fields are just grass and flowers. Nobody is growing any food, and I didn't see any cows or goats. Do you even need to eat?"

Acan grinned at him, the smile of a pleased college professor. "We do eat. Although godlike in our abilities compared to you, we are corporeal beings."

"So what do you eat?" Keshav asked.

Acan shrugged. "We grow mushrooms beneath the city in great numbers. These we treat in a variety of ways."

"A man cannot live on mushrooms alone," Keshav observed.

"I didn't say that was all we ate," Acan said. "And besides, we are not men."

"What's the large structure in the middle?" Doctor Gomez asked.

"It's our public space," Acan said, a little smile on his lips. "For everything. City councils, eating together, civic functions, entertainment rooms. One centralized location for everything you'd do with another person."

Before anyone could say anything to that, they reached the first of the tree-homes. The gnarled, brown wood was stretched as though by magic into a horseshoe shape. The wood was still alive, as evidenced by the bright green leaves growing in bunches from numerous small branches. But it looked polished smooth, as though it had been sanded.

"Which one is yours?" Stuart asked.

"Which one is mine?" Acan repeated slowly, as though trying to answer a riddle. After several moments, his face brightened with realization. "Ah yes. I forget how proprietary you are." He indicated the scattered wooden shelters. "All of these are all of ours. We share in Selvage. Most of them are empty, as we travel or stay for some time in the public space."

"But what's to stop you from just walking into someone else's place?" Stuart asked.

"What's to stop me from walking into you right now?"

"You can see me, for one."

"Exactly."

"Are you telling me that you can sense which of these are occupied and which aren't?" Stuart asked.

"More or less," Acan said. "I find it difficult to explain. But I have an innate sense of where my Selvagian friends are, always. Like knowing which way is up, or recognizing the warmth of fire."

"Interesting," Stuart said. He wasn't sure what else there was to say.

"Now we have traveled for some time," Acan said. He stopped walking and turned to face them. "We have come far today, and from what you told me, you had been going since well before we met. I suggest you get some sleep inside this home."

"I feel fine," Keshav said. "I am not tired at all."

"That would be the *balche*," Acan said. "You above all need some rest."

Keshav nodded.

"While you sleep, I will speak to others about the disc, and your involvement. I will tell you tomorrow what I have learned."

Stuart did feel exhausted. His aching legs, having descended the stairs twice and ascended them once, were wobbling. Since then, he guessed they'd walked at least twenty-five kilometers. Throw in some adrenaline inducing battles and the end result is a kind of weariness that brooks no dissent. And yet, something felt strange. Felt off. Why was Acan so eager to get rid of them?

His eyes drooped, and he was barely aware of Acan opening the doors to a handful of tree houses. "If you grow hungry or wish to bathe, simply step through the portals," Acan said. "All homes are connected to the public space, and you can come through for whatever you need."

The inside was hard for Stuart to focus on. Almost like it had come from, or still partially belonged to, another dimension. The walls were not constant, and there was a feeling of rooms that came and went. The roof at times was just over his head, and at other times, he had the impression of sky above him. He watched this for several long seconds before the room shifted into a semblance of static reality. A basic chamber; one with four walls and a roof and a bed of leaves on the ground. Stuart climbed onto the bed and almost instantly slept the sleep of the dead.

The next day, they were provided with new clothes like that of the natives. The material was more comfortable than anything they'd ever worn, and the patterns were ever-changing spirals of stars. They met other Selvagians. None were gods they had heard of, most claimed their followers had died out long ago. But all were fascinating people with great stories, and friendly tones. A tall woman named Ninkasi seemed to be informally in charge, and as they walked through the city, they were greeted as minor celebrities. Much of the day they spoke with various gentle folk. They explored the public space, eating great plates of steaming mushrooms, and watching a sort of hologram puppet show. Acan showed them a tree-home that was filled with vials of his healing *balche,* spoke to them of the disc, and introduced them to his friend Erinle. Erinle was a muscular brown-skinned man with feminine features; he was apparently also a god of healing. He had a smile that made you want to be his friend. It was a day of rest, of eating, and of new friends.

On their third day, the city was attacked.

***

Acan appeared to them, looking worried. Erinle was by his side. "Please, friends, stay here," Acan said.

"Why? What?" Doctor Gomez asked.

"The forces of Omphalos have appeared in the valley. We will go to repel them."

"Is it?" Doctor Gomez lowered her voice. "Is it Ra?"

Acan didn't say anything, but Erinle nodded. "Close enough," he said, his voice deep. "The Falcon Lord has split himself into two; Authority and Mind. They are leading the forces of Omphalos, and they are opponents both foul and formidable."

Acan grimaced. "Yes, we will need our armor." He turned to the Upworlders. "Remember, stay here. It's for your safety. But you needn't remain ignorant. If we are losing, you should flee, though I cannot guarantee that running away will keep you safe."

He handed them a bamboo cup filled with murky liquid. Mushroom stems and caps bobbed in that dark brew.

Keshav took it. "What do I do with it?"

Acan narrowed his eyes. "Drink it. Just a sip each, if you would see near. More and you will see too much."

Acan and Erinle turned away.

"What does that mean, split himself in two?" Stuart asked.

Before anyone could answer, Erinle turned around. "Mortals," he said. "I can show you, if you would see something marvelous."

Bemused, the four of them followed the two gods. As they moved through the city, Stuart could see, in the distance, a riot of darkness by the mouth of the river. They were too far away from the city in order to see any individuals, but the blogger housed no doubts. "That's them," he hissed.

Doctor Gomez saw them too, and her face crinkled in worry. To have their refuge in this land threatened was a harsh reality to accept.

And then they arrived at a tree-home. It looked much like any other, but when Acan and Erinle opened it, the shining light almost blinded them. The interior was filled with glittering crystal suits. They were incandescent, soft shining blues, greens, pinks, purples, and whites. They stood like silent sentinels, empty vessels of power waiting to be filled.

"These are some of our greatest treasures," Acan said. "At least in the martial realm."

"I can see that," Doctor Gomez said.

"Why would you ever leave the city without them?" Keshav asked.

"We must use them sparingly," Acan admitted. "They need natural light to power them."

"They were designed and created when we still lived on Lemuria," Erinle admitted. "Sunlight was less of a commodity then."

"How do these still even work?" Doctor Gomez asked. "Lemuria sank hundreds of years ago."

"There is an area here, in our land, where the sun shines through the crust of the Earth."

"We're hundreds of feet beneath the Earth's surface. How is that possible?" Stuart said.

Acan shrugged. "I seem to recall we engineered it, long ago, when still we dwelt on the surface. The details aren't important. We recharge our suits there."

"All cities recharge their heliacal technology there," Erinle said, a little awkwardly. "It is the cause of much of our discord with Omphalos."

"Much, but not all," Acan interjected. "Conflict was inevitable."

There was a dark shimmering, and more Selvagians appeared through the portal. Stuart recognized some of them, but he did not remember any of their names apart from Ninkasi. Acan and Erinle joined them, and slowly, with ritualized precision, they donned their crystal armor. Sharp angles jutted from elbows and knees. Quickly, they were completely clad in the crystal armor.

There were two score and ten of them, which claimed about half of the available suits. The armored men and women filed out to the green fields of Selvage. A snorting roar greeted them, and a tall slender woman dressed in verdant robes waited there. Behind her were animals the likes of which they had never seen.

Tall and dark, wide-backed four legged beasts. They looked like moose, but bigger; wild-eyed and more feral. Most of all, their antlers were massive. They were as long as a person; almost two meters of sharp branching horn stretched from their heads.

"What," whispered Stuart to Doctor Gomez, "are *those*?"

Her eyes were wide. Her mouth barely moved as she answered. "Megamoose."

There was a field in a nearby valley, they later learned. The megamoose could wander there, free to graze, rut, and sleep. But there was a tree home there, with one of the teleportation portals. It was the work of mere minutes to gather up the animals, and anyone in Selvage could do it. It took a mighty mount to bear the weight of the crystal clad warriors, and nothing short of a rhino or elephant up on Earth could have handled it. These megamoose were as big as rhinos, even without their antlers.

Out in that field was another creature, even shaggier, even more massive. One that all four of them had seen countless pictures of, even though the animals had been wiped out from the top of the Earth by the early Holocene. They were the mammut; wooly mammoths with shaggy pelts and tusks that stretched from their furry faces. The subtropical temperatures were far too high for the rugged beasts, and they lived in a cooled bubble the Selvagians had created for them. Leaving the temperature controlled bubble even for a short time rapidly fatigued the tundra creatures. It was for this reason alone they were not brought to the battle, for they were sorely needed.

The Selvagians mounted the megamoose and rode off unceremoniously. The four humans were left alone.

"I wish Dean could have seen those," Doctor Gomez said. "Moose were his favorite animals. He had a tattoo of one on his thigh." Her voice was small and her eyes far away.

Stuart was not happy with that image, but for the first time, he realized she must have been falling in love with Dean Maxwell. Already asking herself: *is this the one?* Already thinking about which of her friends would serve as a maid of honor. Already wondering if he wanted children, and what they would name them. Despite the somber mood, Stuart chuckled. Who would have guessed that the analytical, short-tempered Dr. Gomez was a romantic at heart?

All eyes turned on him, and he realized his response was quite inappropriate to Doctor Gomez's statement. To sidestep explaining his train of thoughts, he turned to Keshav, and asked, "What did our friend give you? How will it help you see?"

Keshav hoisted the bamboo tube up into the air. "There's certainly one way to find out." He took a deep drink and passed the elixir to Baruna.

***

Stuart was the last to drink. The brew tasted bitter and earthy. But within moments of ingesting it, Stuart could *see things*. At first he could recognize the tree-homes around them, but from above, the way a sparrow or raven would look upon the world. From there, it took only a little concentration and he could *shift* his perspective. He could still feel his body, bound to the earth on the grass in Selvage. But his consciousness was free, a nomad of the purple sky.

A little experimentation and he was looking down on the invading army of Omphalos. The first thing he noticed was that the army was not made of humans. Nor were there animals present. Instead there were many, two or three hundred, of the shambling creatures. They trod through streams and trampled grass, tore through flower fields, and stomped across shale. The beings were loutish, inhuman. Like robots made out of rocks and mud.

"Do you all see what I see?" Stuart asked. As soon as he thought of them, he was aware of the three others, beside him in the sky.

"I've drunk a lot of chai," Baruna said. "But never has it done *this* to me."

"I get the heebie-jeebies just looking at those things," Doctor Gomez said.

Stuart agreed. "Keshav?" he asked. "Any idea what these are?"

Keshav was silent for some time.

"I wouldn't stake my life on it, but if what I remember from RPGs is correct, I think we'd call them golems."

"Huh," Stuart said. "Well, I don't like the look of them. They're terrifying."

"Well, after you've been swallowed and partially eaten by a plant, terrifying takes on a new meaning," Keshav said. "But at least according to myths, golems are inexorable, unstoppable until they fulfill their purpose."

"Why do I get the feeling," Dr. Gomez asked, "that their purpose involves coming for us?"

Chapter 13

As terrifying as the golem forces were, there was something worse with that army. Clad in white robes, each clasping a nut brown stave, were the twin aspects of Ra: Authority and Mind. They were falcon-faced twins. They moved with a divinely lethal grace and were wrapped in power so strong they shone with it. The only way to tell them apart was that Mind had a red diamond on his forehead; Authority had the same symbol emblazoned on his chest.

"Look at those wankers," Keshav said. The Selvagians were closing in, riding their mighty megamoose at an easy pace. The golems split. Those made mostly of rock and stone shifted to the front, forming a veritable stone wall. The earthy ones jerked to the either side, giving wings to the wall of stone golems. A small brook bubbled merrily behind the terrible beings.

Without breaking their stride, the charging Selvagians shifted into a wedge formation. Acan and Erinle were riding together, over on the left side of the wedge.

Stuart could feel his heart beating quickly, and his mouth felt dry.

"I wanted to go the Maldives for our honeymoon," Baruna said suddenly.

The charging moose accelerated. The golems braced themselves, leaning into the earth itself. Looking as comfortable as two gentlemen strolling across a croquet pitch, the two falconmen held their staves before them.

The air began to crackle with energy. Stuart sensed more than felt a great wash of heat emanating from the staves of Ra's aspects.

Some of the megamoose stumbled from the heat. Three would never rise again, but others struggled to find their footing. The charge faltered, fizzled, but was not finished. With a roar, the Selvagian forces met the golems.

Even with expanded consciousness, it was difficult to see what happened next. Stuart saw the sprawling antlers of the megamoose hit the stone golems. Some golems were torn apart, but so too were many of the antlers snapped, necks broken. The battle became a series of snapshots.

A dismounted warrior in crystal armor charged the two aspects of Ra.

Acan and Erinle rode through earth golems, their steeds trampling enemies into the earth.

The largest stone golem, his hands big as boulders, clapped his hand around the head of an opponent. Even with her crystal helmet, her head, was pancaked and her twitching body fell to the earth.

A dead warrior at the feet of Mind and Authority.

Laser pistols fired into golems, creating holes that quickly sealed up and hurt the golems not at all.

Brown earth and red blood filling the once-clear waters of the brook.

The smell of ozone and blood and smoke and ash and above all, the earthy smell of a summer day just before rain.

The aspect of Ra known as Mind strode forward, his skin turning red with power and energy. His mere touch turned megamoose into cinders, their bodies collapsing in piles of ashes.

Stuart felt his body calling to him, and he realized that the powers of the tea were fading. With an effort that made his head ache, he focused, willing the vision to last as long as it could.

Authority was surrounded by several warriors of Selvage. It struck out against them, but their crystal armor protected them. They pressed in on him, lashing out with blades of crystal and obsidian.

Mind was flame red now. It raised its hand and shot a jet of flame.

The warriors of Selvage began to break, to retreat. But behind Mind one warrior came sprinting in. He plunged his long spear though the head of a golem and sprang through the air.

Mind turned, head cocking upwards.

Too late. Be too late. Stuart pleaded. The vision was going fuzzy, the reception becoming unclear. His eyes watered with the effort of watching. Already he could sense that Keshav and Doctor Gomez were gone, back in their bodies.

The charging Selvagian, while still in mid-air, pulled out a blade and drove it through the head of Mind. The falcon-headed creature crumpled to the ground. His skin bleached color, returning to snow white in the matter of seconds. But it was not dead. It stood and raised its stave at the Selvagian warrior.

"Stuart," someone was saying. "Stuart."

For a moment, Stuart could see the concerned faces of his companions. He was sitting cross-legged on the grass, and his legs were asleep. With a great effort of will, he closed his eyes, and his consciousness escaped for one more moment.

Mind was bleeding and running away. Authority limped over to aid him. The golems were broken, lumps of earth and stone, possessing no sentience whatsoever.

The remaining Selvagians were gathering their steeds and returning to the city. They had won. Only then did Stuart return to his body.

***

That night, they ate in the public hall. It was both celebration and wake for those who had fallen. Tall pitchers of brown, green, and blue beverages were stacked on tree trunks. On another, plates filled with sizzling mushrooms awaited. Stuart sat next to Keshav and Baruna. He looked expectantly for their fourth, but when she joined them, Doctor Gomez sat next to a thin Selvagian man whose long brown hair was gathered into a ponytail. All Selvagians were wiry and tall, but this fellow was damn near gangly. He would have been a comic figure had he not possessed the grace and bearing of a demi-god. A grace that was somewhat belied by the scruffy goatee he wore, calling to Stuart's mind images of Florida trailer park trash.

Nala, he was called. And soon he had Doctor Gomez laughing at every little comment he whispered to her. He told loud tales of his prowess; it had been he who had wounded the aspect of Ra known as Mind.

Stuart watched them; the mushrooms tasted like acid in his stomach.

"It is hard to see, is it not?" Keshav said softly. "If it helps, she is not for you. You know this somewhere, I think."

"Yes, that really does help. Thanks so much," Stuart said, sarcasm not hidden one bit.

Keshav ignored his tone. "This is why I married. I did not know Baruna beforehand, but the problems of marriage are better than the alienation of being single."

Stuart was surprised enough that he forgot his clenching jealousy. "You were an arranged marriage?" The Selvagian next to him passed him a pitcher full of blue liquid and Stuart filled his cup. It tasted of fennel and rosemary. He couldn't say if it was alcoholic or not.

"Of course," Keshav laughed. He nodded to Baruna, but like most of the others, she was absorbed by Nala's story of the battle. "It still happens today. It's as good or better a system as love, believe it or not."

"I don't believe it," Stuart said.

"That's what you've been trained to believe," Keshav countered. "Think about it. My parents know me better than anyone. They have searched for someone suitable for me for all of my life. Oh they may very well be wrong, but we're talking about an informed decision." Here he emphasized the word *decision*. "One made by two people who love me and understand me. How does that compare with some chemical reaction in your body that you yourself don't even understand?"

"Love is more than a chemical reaction," Stuart protested.

Keshav cocked an eyebrow at him.

"It is," Stuart repeated. He didn't know how he knew this, but know it he did. "Though I admit you and Baruna are well-matched."

"We are well along the road to love," Keshav agreed. "But it takes work. Though I am a Sikh, and all that that entails, I am also an Englishmen. I have never lived in India."

"Have you been there?"

"Once," Keshav said. "I found it a challenging place. They tell you to expect the unexpected, but though I was not troubled by touts, and I grew use to the starving animals and shit in the streets, I could not accept the starving children and old men. Death is held away from us in the west. In India, you see it every day. Death is life there."

Stuart wondered idly about interviewing Keshav for his blog. The man was eloquent.

"But that's not the point. I am Indian, and I am English. Two men in one. It is similar with Baruna. I am me, Keshav. But I am also Keshav and Baruna. Do you see?"

Stuart was not able to reply. Nala stood then, his eyes meeting everyone there. "And the only way I survived," he said, raising his voice so that all could hear him. "Is because I train every morning, running to the valley of the moose and back without rest. There is no greatness without fitness." His ponytail flounced as he proclaimed this.

It was oddly encouraging to Stuart that even here, in a city of gods at the center of the Earth, there were still douchebags.

***

After the dinner, when most everyone had left, Stuart was mulling over Keshav's words. Two men in one. How many men was Stuart? Just one, surely. Was that his problem?

Stuart rose and walked through a portal to an empty tree-home. Once inside, however, he didn't feel like sleeping. He slipped out the front entrance and walked around the city. A few people were out, but it appeared most were sleeping, though it remained as light as ever. He didn't see Acan until he bumped into him.

Acan smiled. "Great thoughts for great minds?"

Stuart smiled. "Something like that."

"The battle today was unlike any we have had for some time. We here at Selvage are something like a collective. None of us have power over the others, apart from the power of persuasion. Not even Ninkasi can command us against our will. But Omphalos is different. He of two horizons is the lord of the city. He holds absolute power. For all of that, he rarely intervenes personally. Sending his aspect to us today was a marked message." He paused for a moment. "You saw the battle today? Your inner eye was clear?"

"Yes," Stuart said. "What was in that beverage?"

"Mushrooms and fungus of a powerful nature, ones that free your consciousness. You have something like it on the crust, but those are merely a fraction the potency, a campfire compared to a sunset, and the crop has been twisted so that many see evil and wrongness."

"You gave us magic mushrooms?" Stuart asked. He had never done drugs before.

"There was nothing magic about them, though it is an amusing name. You should get some sleep. The next few days may be taxing."

"I'm not tired," Stuart said. "And why taxing?"

"We need something of you," Acan said.

The evasion bothered Stuart. "Listen, there are sick and dying people waiting for us. Dozens of them. If you can help us get back, it needs to be soon."

Acan looked mournful. "We lost twelve men today, eight women, and two score of our animal friends. And that was against just a finger of strength from Omphalos. We drained most of the power from half of our armor. If we fight them for the power of the sun, their forces will be far stronger, and we will be weaker. And you should know this. Those golems today. They came for you."

"How does Ra even know we are here?" Stuart asked.

"Those men who almost killed me served him. They will have informed upon your arrival. Besides, though he of two horizons may not be omniscient in the strictest sense of the word, he has a good idea of what happens in his realm."

"What does he want with us?" Stuart asked.

Acan held his hands up. "I cannot guess. He is very interested in those from the above realms. Those of the below as well."

Below? Stuart thought, but before he could ask, Acan continued.

"They were not here solely for you, of course. Twenty Selvagians would not have died if that were the case. He also seeks to protect the sun disc."

"I'm sorry for your losses," Stuart said, feeling helpless. "We didn't ask for any of them to fight."

Acan shrugged. "I know. The falcon lord has the sun disc. With its power, we are poorly matched."

"How can we help?"

"We need an ally. Selvage is a great city, Ompahlos, for all the flaws of autocracy, is an even greater. There are other, smaller communities. Ek Chuaj lives in one such place. But there is a third great city: Graben. You can help by traveling there and enlisting their aid."

"You have portals in your homes. Why don't you just teleport there?"

"It's not that easy. The Grabens are aloof, they do not take sides, and they do not approve us or of Omphalos. They cut off communication with us long ago."

"So we are to be your intermediary?" Stuart asked.

Acan nodded. "It will be dangerous. Many are the perils of our world for those of your weaknesses. Even if you do make it to their stone city, there is no telling what you may find. They may not let you into their city at all. It has been a long time since an outsider has visited Graben. But the fact remains. If you want to return to your home world, you'll need the sun disc. If we are to free it from Omphalos, you'll need the help of the greatest of cities."

"And we have to do this?"

"Not at all. It only becomes necessary if you ever want to return to the surface world."

Stuart rubbed his hair in frustration. "I see. Thank you for explaining."

Acan bid him farewell soon after. Stuart walked around for some time more. His head was full of questions and problems, but it felt good to have a direction. He started humming something that only after a while did he realize was a *White Stripes* tune. But something like an hour later, when he finally returned to the tree-home assigned to him, he saw Doctor Gomez and Nala entering her home together.

Chapter 14

It wasn't really the next day, but everyone had slept, or otherwise been occupied, for seven or so hours when they met again. There was no way to tell how much time had passed, but if felt like more than five hours and less than ten. Acan gathered them together and brought them into the large public tree-home. They entered a room they had not seen before, a leafy green chamber with red flowers sprouting along the walls like wallpaper. Acan explained to them all what he and Stuart had discussed the previous night. This time he went into more detail, explaining that with the sun disc they could achieve any number of great things.

"It can certainly create a portal between our world and yours," he said. "That will be the easy part, once we have the sun disc."

"How did we get here?" Doctor Gomez asked. "A cave just appeared in front of us."

"This happens," Acan said. "More so in places like Antarctica, the Bermuda Triangle, Siberia, Göbekli Tepe. The fabric of reality is stretched there, and natural laws don't always flow the way they do elsewhere."

Stuart thought of the different stars, of his floating body. He wondered if that also explained things like alien sightings, ghosts recorded on film, and other inexplicable phenomena.

"Now," Acan said, gesturing to a stump piled up with clothing and supplies. "I have provided you with food, and some of the pistols you saw the day you rescued me. What's more, I have cloaks here, cool in the heat, but will warm you in frigid conditions. Best of all, I have a pair of wandering boots for each of you."

"Why can't we just teleport through one of the portals?" Keshav asked.

Stuart loaded his backpack up with food and a pistol. It made it heavier than he would like, but he'd prefer a little inconvenience if it meant being better prepared.

Acan looked at him blankly and then laughed. "Of course, you don't know. The portals are Selvagian technology. They need to be linked, connected, *grown*. The people of Graben would never consent to our building a portal into their city. I'm afraid it will be a long journey, but one my gifts will help."

He had the proprietary manner of a lecturer, and it reminded Stuart of his dream, back on the cruise ship. These gods were dinosaurs, in a certain sense.

"What do the boots do?" Stuart asked. From where he sat, they looked like any old pair of hiking boots.

"They will carry you thrice as fast as your natural speed. Your feet will never tire. Your toes will never blister. When pointed at a target the wandering boots will carry you there, and you cannot get lost."

"What are they made of?" Keshav asked. "We cannot wear leather," his voice was apologetic, but steady.

"Haven't you guessed?" Acan asked. "I have not made this so much as grown them. The primary substance, is of course, fungus. They will help greatly on your journey."

"You speak as though you're not going to be there. Aren't you coming with us?" Stuart asked.

Acan's face fell. "Alas, I cannot. After our losses yesterday, we need all of us here to defend Selvage. I am no fighter, but my healing is necessary. Should the Falcon Lord attack again, we need to be ready."

"We, we will not be alone," Doctor Gomez said. "Nala said he would accompany us."

Acan's eyes flashed. "That is most unwise of him," he said. "Though it is ultimately his decision to do as he wishes."

"What is Nala the god of?" Keshav asked.

All eyes turned to Doctor Gomez. "I actually have no idea," she said, but a little smile on her lips suggested this was a restrained answer.

"He was not known by one name in your realm," Acan said. "He is a minor aspect of speed, a Hermes-light."

"They won't let him into the city either, right?" Stuart asked.

"That is not for me to say," Acan said. "Though his aid in the first leg of your journey will be helpful."

"Helpful why?" Stuart asked.

"What is the first leg of our journey?" Keshav asked.

"I don't think the two Aspects will be looking for you. I do suspect they wanted to capture you during the battle, but I don't think that was their primary purpose. Nala will provide you some protection in case I am wrong. As to the other," Acan hesitated, a little reluctant to answer, "it isn't as bad as it sounds."

"Where are we going?" Stuart asked.

"You must sail across the Sea of Monsters," Acan said.

***

Their boat was a simple craft, powered by the wind, and technologies they could only guess at. Nala sat at the helm, his hands alternately touching a series of four crystals. The Sea of Monsters was glittering blue and stunningly beautiful. If there were monsters, none had shown themselves yet. It felt like they were sailing on the Aegean, or through the South Pacific.

They had traveled through a tangled mangrove swamp to reach the sea. The wandering boots really were wonderful, shedding sucking mud, and giving them the pace of a run with only the effort a casual stroll. They had seen large animals prowling the swamp; a Volkswagen sized armadillo with a spiked club tail that looked like it could shatter through a castle wall. These had been peaceful, grazing animals. Worse were the cats; lanky, sneaking creatures that had stalked them until Nala had shot one with his laser pistol. The one he killed did not have long fangs, but Stuart suspected he had seen a few saber-toothed cats in the bushes. Watching them with the infinite patience of the hunter. Some preternatural sense warned him that he was being hunted, but they had made it to the boat without further violence.

"Are there any deserts in this land?" Doctor Gomez asked. She was sitting next to Nala, who was dressed in a red vest tunic, leaving most of his legs, arms, and hairy chest visible.

"There are," he said. His voice was high and belied his muscular frame. "Omphalos squats in a wasteland, a dry rotting desert of rolling dunes. South of Selvage is another, a high desert, with scrub brush, cold nights, and lurking scavengers. Why do you ask?"

"Well," she said, musing. "I'm thinking about those armadillos we saw. They were massive.

"What does that have to do with deserts?" Baruna asked.

"As continents get drier, forests disappear. The open plains spread and, over time, that gives animals room to grow larger. It explains some of the creatures we've seen here."

Nala laughed heartily. "Those things may be true in your world. I assure you they are not here. With the power of the sun disc, Ra could boil an ocean away, creating overnight a wasteland that he could populate with terrifying creatures."

"Is that supposed to make us feel better?" Keshav asked.

"The truth rarely does, especially for lesser life forms."

"Hey," Keshav said, his tone light.

Nala shrugged. "We are gods. You are not. Do you expect rabbits or ants to understand the world around you?"

Keshav scowled, and Baruna stroked his arm. "It's not worth it, *jaanu*." she said.

"I've had the misfortune of dealing with some right wankers," he said, loud enough that it was clear he wasn't only addressing Baruna. "But this guy is well up there."

"What's that?" Stuart asked. He had been watching the sea, lost in thoughts. Now, however, on the horizon he could see … *something*.

The others looked two, eyes squinted in concentration.

"Well," Nala said. "This is ill luck indeed."

"What is it?" Doctor Gomez asked. "They look like clouds."

"They're sails," Nala answered. "Two of them. Unless I miss my guess, and I never do, they are the boats Mandjet and Mesektet."

"That sounds familiar," Doctor Gomez said.

"It should," Nala said. "They are the boats of the two aspects of the Falcon Lord. He must be angry for the blow I struck against him. They are coming for me, surely as leeches after a rain."

"Inconceivable," Stuart said. No one laughed. No one ever laughed at his jokes.

There was silence for some time. "Turds! We can turn around," Baruna said. "We are not too far from the shore."

"We could," Nala said. "They would catch us. Their ships are as fast as a winter sunrise, as steady as a twinkling star. Even if not, we would have to report home as failures. The next attack, or the one after that, could utterly destroy us forever."

"So we push on?" Doctor Gomez said. "Can we get this ship to go any faster?"

"Can you make the wind blow harder?" Nala asked sarcastically. His ponytail bounced a little as he scowled. "I shouldn't have come. I've endangered you all, and simply because I underestimated just how badly the Sun Lord would want to revenge himself."

"You almost killed one of them yesterday," Doctor Gomez said.

"Yesterday I had my armor. Yesterday we had our mighty steeds, and I had the companionship of my peers. Today I am babysitting lesser creatures." His eyes fell on them as the tirade trailed out. He put his arm around Doctor Gomez's shoulder. Stuart half expected her to shake it off, but instead, she snuggled more closely into his body.

"It's worth it, of course," Nala said to her. "To be with you. And someone has to look out for these puny humans."

"We were doing fine before you came along," Stuart said, feeling acid in his stomach again. Why was he so bothered? He had no claim on Doctor Gomez, and having Nala along gave them a great sense of security.

Nala looked at him the way you look at a child who tells you he can fly or turn invisible. His silent reproach was more eloquent than any words.

But Stuart had had enough. "You can go home now, for all we care!"

"Stuart," Doctor Gomez admonished.

"Acan said it was foolish for him to come along," Stuart said.

"Acan," Nala said. "That bent potion brewer? He prefers the company of men to women. How can you take anything that pervert says seriously?"

"Sorry to interrupt," Baruna said. "I think we might have even bigger problems." She pointed into the water.

Instantly everyone peered over the side. The water was clear, and they could see the creature beneath them. It had four legs and swam at a great pace; certainly faster than their craft. It looked like a pig crossed with an elephant and hippo. It was large, enormously large.

"What the hell is that?" Stuart asked.

"I think it's a Myratherium ," Doctor Gomez said.

"Is that what you call them?" Nala said. "A clumsy name for a clumsy animal. But it is no threat to us. They are large enough that even sharks and crocodiles will not bother it. But they are gentle creatures for all their size."

"I wasn't talking about the swimming pig-elephant," Baruna said, her voice a little cross. "I was talking about *that*."

Stuart looked again. Swimming up from under the Myratherium was a true monster. It looked like an orca crossed with the loch ness monster, but it was far larger than either. Something like four times longer than a great white, it must have weighed several tons.

"Basilosaurus," Doctor Gomez said. "I never had any idea I would be meeting so many of these creatures."

"A gamachus," Nala grunted. "Ill luck to meet one here."

"Can we shoot it?" Doctor Gomez asked.

"A creature that size?" Nala said. "It will just make him angry. And that goes double for our divine enemies."

As they all stared in transfixed horror, the monster swam up, and took a tremendous bite out of the swimming pig-elephant. Even the Basilosaurus was not large enough to swallow a Myratherium whole. But half of the creature was gone, and the cool water was suddenly murky with warm blood.

"What's to stop him from coming after our boat?" Stuart asked, horrified.

The Basilosaurus snapped its jaws shut again, all that remained of the peaceful Myratherium was blood in the water, and a few scraps of food. Stuart reached for his pistol.

"Forget it, I said," Nala said. "These pistols are powerful, but they would only serve to anger the gamachus."

"Next time some wanker suggests we go into the sea of monsters," Keshav said. "I'm going to give it a miss."

"The sails are coming closer," Stuart said. "Much closer." In a short time, the ships of Ra had closed over half the distance. They were close enough now that their shape was clear: long canoes with a high prow. Mind and Authority were just visible, holding their staves into the air as though powering their craft with magic and will. The ships shimmered and were suddenly only meters away.

It was then, as all stared at the approaching baleful gods, that the Basilosaurus struck.

Chapter 15

Their ship was stronger than it looked, and the mighty monster of the sea did not hit them as hard as it might have. But it was enough. The vessel flew into the air; one meter high, then two. Stuart saw the impassive faces of Ra's aspects, turned up mutely as they watched the boat soar into the sky.

They came down with a whoosh and a splash. The water was warm as it coated them all. Some lake weed landed in Nala's goatee, and he scowled as he picked at the slippery stuff. Baruna halfway fell out, and it took some scrambling from Stuart and Keshav to pull her back into the boat. Meager though it was, the protection of the boat was vastly preferable to the naked vulnerability of the water.

Nala drew his sword. "I'm going to fight them," he said. "Try not to get eaten alive by the gamachus." He leapt from the boat, almost capsizing it, and sprang through the air. The boats Mandjet and Mesektet were four meters away, but Nala cleared the distance easily. He landed to face the two falcon-headed enemies.

The Basilosaurus was silent and unseen. Stuart glanced down and saw nothing beneath them. A bright flash of red brought his attention back the battle of demigods.

Nala was fast with his sword. He moved in blurry jerks, too fast for their human eyes to follow.

Mind and Authority, for now they stood side by side on the Mandjet, were slower, more methodical. But for each hyper-quick sword slash, every cut and stroke of Nala's sword, they parried with their heavy staves. Nalas's growl of frustration was audible across the water.

"What do we do?" Baruna asked.

"Where is that damn fish?" Stuart asked.

"It's not a fish," Dr. Gomez said.

"Whatever! It's the only thing currently trying to eat us," Stuart said. "Let's get this boat going, head toward land."

"Not without Nala," Doctor Gomez said. She crossed her arms against her chest.

"Did you see him jump?" Stuart said. "He'll be fine. It's us that we need to be worried about." That sounded plausible, but Stuart didn't kid himself. He'd be happy never seeing Nala again.

The two parts of Ra were getting the better of Nala. He was now on the defensive, ponytail bouncing as he parried attacks from both of his opponents. Their ships were much larger, their sails much wider and broader than the Selvagian craft the four of them sat in. But mightier though they were, they shook as the Basilosaurus emerged from under them.

"It's over there now," Keshav said.

"We should go," Baruna said.

Stuart was already at the helm. He moved his hands across the crystals.

"I can't just leave him," Dr. Gomez said. "*We* can't just leave him. You should know better than that."

Stuart found that touching the crystals on the right and the left and pressing forward on them made the craft leap forward.

"Too late now," he said. "We're going forward."

A roar made all of them look back. The sea monster reared its head, screaming an animal challenge at the men below it. It was massive, with a long snout full of sharp teeth. Apart from the sail and mast, it could almost certainly swallow the Mandjet or Mesektet whole. Instead it struck down, smashing the Mesektet into slivers of flotsam and jetsam.

"*Pendejos*," Dr. Gomez said. "You know the right thing to do."

"He said to avoid the monster," Stuart said. "That's exactly what we're doing." Their little craft was picking up speed now, really skipping over the waves.

The Basilosaurus snapped at Authority. The falcon-headed man sidestepped it. As the sea monster pulled its head back, aiming another strike at it, Authority raised his staff. A bright flame flowered from the tip, engulfing the monster and, within a few heartbeats, the creature was reduced to scattered ashes.

"Fuck's sake," Keshav breathed. "I was afraid of the wrong monster."

Nala took advantage of the distraction and struck his long blade into Mind's leg. The creature did not react to pain or from the force of the blow. It struck out again with its stave. Nala leapt away, back into the water. Halfway into his jump, he twisted, turning it into a dive. His body sunk into the water and did not visibly emerge in the next several moments.

Neither of the aspects of Ra paid him any heed. Mind bent down, removed the blade that remained stuck in its leg, and cast it into the sparkling blue sea. The two of them on one ship now, they began to sail forward, toward the Upworlders.

"Faster," Keshav said. They had a small head start, but not one that would matter against these powerful entities.

Stuart pressed down on one of the middle crystals. The boat slowed dangerously. He moved his hand the other way, pulling up on the crystal. The boat sped up.

Keshav cheered.

Baruna did not. "We're leaking," she said, panic rising in her voice. "Look at the bottom of the boat."

Stuart glanced from the horizon. He thought he could see land there, vague on the horizon. But now his gaze moved to the bottom of their ship.

Baruna was right. The boat had been damaged by the initial attack, and now the high speed it sailed at further weakened the frame. Water burbled in a long thin line small enough that the eye could not see it. Judging from the line of water, though, the crack was at least a meter-and-a-half-long.

"We can't stop now," Stuart said.

"Keep going," Doctor Gomez said. "Go faster. We'll swim the last way there if we need to."

"The ship will break in two," Keshav said. "That's what a hairline fracture will do."

Despite himself, Stuart smiled at the orange turbaned man's inadvertent rhyme. He pushed up on the crystal, willing the ship to go faster.

The horizon approached rapidly. Blurring distant objects began to resolve themselves as trees, boulders, and stone fortifications. But their boat was now full of water, suffering from a too-high speed. Worse, the Mandjet was quickly catching up with them. Everyone stared as the two aspects of Ra drew closer, propelled by sorcery. They were no more than two meters away.

A voice sounded, in their boat. It didn't belong to any of them. "Citizens of the upper world," it said, in a voice that sparkled, shiny and rich with timbre. "Do not flee. We mean no harm. I mean no harm."

The four of them frowned together. There was something convincing about the voice, the paternal assurances filling their heads, their minds with calm confidence.

The ships hurtled toward the shore as the four of them stared at each other, uncertainty blooming in their eyes. The boat began to vibrate, as though being shaken by a giant. This seemed to break the spell of Ra's voice, and it seemed like the air was again clear.

"I'm not being funny," Keshav said. "But I think our boat is about to sink."

Chapter 16

The water was warm and buoyant, as comfortable as a bath after a long day in the snow. Stuart had taken the boat as far as he could, but they were still a hundred meters or more from the shore; it was hard to estimate, but now the pine trees and stone walls were much closer, much larger. All of them had splashed into the water as the boat gurgled and sank. With it went their provisions, their gear, their way back to Omphalos.

The worry now, however, was getting to the shore without being attacked by whatever might be lurking in the water. The two aspects of Ra sailed to the shore where they unhurriedly left their boat and waited on land. They could afford to wait for the humans.

Keshav swam to help Baruna, who was not a strong swimmer.

Doctor Gomez was in fact an excellent swimmer, and she swam with confident sure strokes, outdistancing them all.

Stuart stayed back with Keshav and Baruna, knowing that his help could be needed. First, however, he needed to know if they were safe. He plunged his head into the salty water and opened his eyes. It stung, but the water was clear enough that he could see all around him. No sign of big monsters. No sign of anything, save for some tendrils of lake weed floating close to the shore.

Stuart emerged. "Coast is clear," he gasped. "Come on."

Baruna was stolidly doggy paddling and Keshav swam next to her.

It was slow going, and Doctor Gomez reached the shore well before them.

Neither of the aspects of Ra approached her, but Stuart thought he could hear a faint murmuring from afar, almost like the buzzing of bees.

Doctor Gomez, leaning on a tall tree to catch her breath, had a wondering expression in her eyes.

The trio was three meters away, bobbing in the warm salt water and almost close enough to touch the bottom, when something grabbed Stuart's leg.

He panicked, kicking, and thrashing. His head sunk under as the force on his leg pulled at him. His last vision was the purple sky, and Keshav's concerned expression.

Once under, he saw exactly what had happened. Swimming low to the ground, his hands still on Stuart's leg, was Nala. He raised one hand to his lips, while the other clutched at lakeweed to him close the bottom. *Shhhh.* Stuart nodded emphatically, his lungs burning.

Still the man didn't let go. He pointed towards the shore and made an elaborate gesture with his hand. Stuart had no idea what it meant but he nodded emphatically. He hadn't much time left before expelling the last bit of air.

Nala did not let go. He continued to make the same gesture with his hand, opening and closing two of his fingers, tapping them into his thumb. Stuart's breath expelled in a burst, and he kicked at Nala. At last the man understood and relinquished his grip.

Warm salty water filled Stuart's lungs, and he emerged coughing and hacking. As he gradually regained control of his body and wiped the water from his eyes, it was evident that everyone had reached the shore.

The two aspects of Ra stood some distance away; they remained closer to their ship than the wet trio of humans. The remnants of a stone wall stretched behind them all, culminating in a crumbling tower as tall as four men.

Stuart's feet found purchase, and he scrambled up the shore, still coughing out water from his lungs. "I'm alright," he said. His new clothes dried instantly as they met air. His backpack, made of Earthly material, was wet and had come unzipped. Anything could have fallen out, but just as he checked, he was interrupted.

"Greetings," a stereophonic voice said. It was in the air all around them, as if it came from invisible speakers. "There are things you must learn about our world. My world. Selvage and Omphalos are."

At this moment, Nala sprang from the water, and interrupted the interrupters. He was unarmed but he launched himself at the two aspects of Ra. Their falcon faces betrayed no surprise, but he managed to attack them before they raised their staffs.

Stuart rushed to the others. He still had no idea what Nala had said, but he wasn't above faking it. "Come on," he said. "We have to get away. Nala told me so, underwater."

The pony-tailed Selvagian was using his fists, his elbows, his knees, and feet in an intricate dance. Mind and Authority were moving in conjunction, but he was too fast for them.

"But," Doctor Gomez said.

"Hurry!" Stuart said. "There's no time."

He physically pushed them away, toward the trees, and away from the shore.

"We cannot help him now, Doctor Gomez," Keshav said.

Doctor Gomez reluctantly followed as they fled into away from the battle. They ran blindly, sprinting and leaping over stones, dodging trees, bounding over roots embedded in the moist earth. After some time, they came to gasping halt to catch their breaths.

"What happened to those laser pistols?" Keshav asked. "One might come in handy about now."

Stuart reached for his in his backpack, but it had fallen out at some point in his escape from the boat.

"Anyone else got one?" Keshav asked. "It might mean the difference between life and death."

They all shook their heads no, not a little forlornly.

"Run for our lives it is," Stuart said. The prospect did not excite him.

"Wait," Doctor Gomez said. She panted, and a trickle of sweat dropped down her face. "These stones," she said. "Remember what Acan did?" She pushed one stone on top of another.

Stuart looked to Keshav and Baruna in askance, but he received merely blank looks.

"I must admit," Baruna said softly. "I am curious as to what the two gods want to say."

"You mean like they are the good guys and they're trying to warn us that we've sided with the wrong team?" Keshav said. "Yeah I was a little a little worried about that too."

"Help. Me," Doctor Gomez said, teeth gritted in concentration. She struggled with a stone far too big for her to lift.

Stuart belatedly realized what she was doing. "You can't be serious."

Her look was a snarl, and Stuart bent to pick up the third stone. Keshav came to help too, and a moment later so did Baruna.

With a massive effort, they lifted the stone waste high and rolled it onto the other two boulders.

"I want to go on record as saying this is a bad idea," Stuart said. "Please don't do it."

Doctor Gomez did not even hear him. She reached into her pocket and pulled out the last section of a chocolate bar.

"Hang on," Keshav said. "You've been holding out. I could go for a bit of chocolate."

Doctor Gomez ignored him too. She placed the smooshed, wet, melted chocolate on top of the third stone, and muttered something.

Stuart stared in amazement. Somehow she knew the words! There was a shimmering haze. When it cleared, a man stood there. It was, of course, Ek Chuaj. He remained striped black and white, humanoid but for the scorpion tail behind him. His long spear was in one hand, and the red woolen sack remained slung over his right shoulder. The smell of chocolate was once more in the air.

His eyes flashed in anger as he beheld them.

"How dare you. How dare you bid me here. You boundless apes." He drew himself up angrily, gathering himself in.

"Honored Ek Chuaj," Doctor Gomez said, prostrating herself. "I would not have dared but the need is great." She stood but kept her head lowered respectfully.

Stuart and the others followed suit.

"I know your enemy," he said. "And I have no wish for him to be mine as well."

"Our enemy now is not the sun lord himself, but his aspects, the two falcon men."

Ek Chuaj's arm fell. For the first time, his face reflected something other than anger. "Hu and Sia? They walk the inner Earth again?"

Something loud crashed through the forest. Stuart glanced back nervously but didn't see anything yet. "Hurry," he said to Doctor Gomez.

"Indeed they do," Doctor Gomez said. "They are near to us, and without your aid, we have no chance."

Stuart cursed. Was that the best she could do?

The striped god frowned. "I owe a debt to those two, and would welcome a chance to test myself against them. However, your sacrifice was paltry. There is cow milk and insects and chemicals and sea water in the cacao you have offered me."

The crashing was much louder, much closer now. Footsteps pounded, and Stuart could hear heavy breathing.

"American chocolate isn't what it could be," Doctor Gomez admitted. "If you can help us survive, I will take back with me some of your cacao and show the world what true cacao was meant to be. Furthermore, I will fly to Switzerland, and sacrifice the finest chocolate known to man in your honor."

"It's meant to be drunk," Ek Chuaj said. He hefted his spear. "Very well, I accept your paltry terms."

He had not finished speaking when Nala burst through the trees. He sprinted toward them, eyes wild, and skin charred and burnt in patches. "Why have you stopped? Run! They are too strong!" he shouted wildly.

Nala skidded to a stop when he realized Ek Chuaj was there. He looked back and forth from Ek Chuaj to Doctor Gomez, as though he couldn't believe his eyes. "How is this possible?"

Ek Chuaj nodded once, solemnly, to him. One warrior greeting another. He raised his spear in the air.

And then a burst of flame shot through the air. It just missed Nala, and instead hit a lone palm tree, instantly darkening the tough wood.

Mind and Authority stepped slowly into view. They were stalking Nala, like a jaguar, but when they saw Ek Chuaj there, spear raised, they both stopped. The striped god growled a warning at them.

"I don't understand," Keshav said. "Why he will fight aspects of Ra but not Ra himself.

"Who's to know why a god does anything?" Baruna said.

"I imagine it's a bit like stepping on two ants instead of trying to stamp out an entire anthill," Doctor Gomez said.

"Yeah, but if stepping on two ants incites the entire anthill, it's not such a good idea."

"We should probably go now," Keshav said.

Nala reached them, still out of breath and body bruising from countless hits. Most of his goatee was burnt off.

The aspects of Ra remained where they had stopped. Motionless, they almost blended in with the background. Their hawk eyes stared keenly at the god of chocolate and war.

"I'm with you," Stuart said. Baruna nodded, wide-eyed.

"He can catch up," Doctor Gomez said, after a moment's hesitation.

Before any of them had so much as taken a step, Ek Chuaj manifested before the two aspects of Ra. One moment he was beside them and, quick as blinking, the next he was not. He lunged at Mind and Authority so quickly there was no time to react.

The point of his spear sunk deeply into the belly of Authority. They all watched, transfixed, as the manifestation of Ra sunk to the ground. His staff fell from his limp fingers.

Stuart instinctively ran toward the fight.

The striped god used his spear as a staff, blocking the powerful strikes from Mind.

Authority had both hands over the gaping wound in his stomach, and his skin began to shimmer.

Stuart was two steps away from the fallen deity when a hand clasped his shoulder. Nala stood behind him, his strong arms completely arresting all notion.

"Let me go," Stuart said. He could see the staff lying on the ground.

Nala had misunderstood though. "I don't know what they said to you. But you will not aid them."

"I'm not going to help them, you dumbass!" Stuart said. "Let go of me."

"Not possible. I will not let you make a mistake."

The others had not left. They were transfixed, watching the duel of the deities. Keshav motioned with his hand, like to a dog. *Come here.*

Ek Chauj used his scorpion tail, flicking it at his enemy, to keep him at bay, but he was losing the battle, and he took several steps back. Mind swole with power, and his speed and strength grew by the moment. Even with tail and spear, Ek Chuaj was outmatched.

"Don't you see?" Nala said. "With only one manifestation, he will have more of Ra's power. Nothing can stop him now."

Mind shot a blast of flame at Ek Chuaj, who barely dodged. The creature of Ra was then on him, swinging his heavy staff so quickly that Stuart could not follow the motion.

"All right," Stuart said. "No need to carry me. I'll go back." Nala did not relax his grip. "Good," he said. "Hurry."

"Oh," Stuart said, "just one thing."

Stuart had never punched a man in the dick before, but he figured it would be a good time to try. Nala was tall enough that he didn't have to do much but punch forward, and it took the Selvagian completely by surprise. He doubled over and fell to the ground. *Corporeal beings indeed*, Stuart thought.

Stuart broke free and grabbed the fallen staff. Authority's body faded, almost gone now, as it vanished into a ghost-like form. Ten paces in front of him, Ek Chuaj was on his back, his spear broken in two, his scorpion tail cracked and limp. Mind was glowing now, filled with starlight. He raised his staff above his head, holding onto it with both hands.

Ek Chuaj disappeared for a moment and then returned to the same place. From where he stood, Stuart saw the surprise on his face. And then light so hot and so bright poured into the striped god. His body began to melt away.

"No," Stuart cried. He aimed the captured staff and, concentrating, sent a burst of fire at Mind.

The manifestation of Ra was caught completely unaware as the blast hit it in the head. It howled in pain, and the smell of burnt feathers filled the air. The creature leapt forward and aimed its staff at Stuart.

Just then, Nala stood. "You'll pay for that, little mortal," he said.

Stuart realized there was no apologizing, no rationale for what he'd done. Not to someone like this. He tried anyway.

"Listen, dude," he started. Mind had taken two more steps and Stuart winced, anticipating the heat of the attack.

Nala took two steps toward him, anger blinding him to everything but his target.

Fire hit the tall Selvagian, and his body, instantly, was merely ashes floating to the ground.

Stuart readied the staff and shot another blast at Mind, just missing. The aspect of Ra hissed, and then leapt in the air. Stuart watched the fleeing creature soar away for a long time, until it was merely a speck on the horizon.

He didn't even know he was shaking until he felt arms around him. "Group hug," Keshav announced, his voice full of false cheer.

Doctor Gomez and Baruna were there too, and they held him until his body stopped shaking. Their bodies felt warm, and the touch of humans helped his heart stop beating so quickly.

Stuart flung the staff away from him. It skittered onto the ground and came to a rest beneath a small fern.

Doctor Gomez went to see the remains of Ek Chuaj.

"I'm sorry," Stuart said. His voice was harsh with emotion. "I got him killed."

"That's nonsense, mate. You might have saved us all," Keshav said.

"Guys," Doctor Gomez said. She was kneeling down in front of the striped god. "Come here for a second."

They found Ek Chuaj still breathing. His breathing was a steam train, his body half burnt off, but he seemed happy.

"I got one of them," he said. "Ek Chuaj remains the most mighty."

"Can we help you?" Doctor Gomez asked.

Ponderously, with great effort, Ek Chuaj shook his head no. "I am not dead. Nor dying. It takes more than that to kill me. But I must withdraw for some time. I will return to you. I will not forget our bargain."

"I won't either," Doctor Gomez assured him.

The deity's body slid away, became insubstantial, seeped into the ground, soared into the air, and was gone.

There was nothing to be done with Nala's remains. A few ashes floated in the air, like snowflakes, but the man was gone. Even though he had been a prick, he'd certainly been brave, and had done well to protect them. Stuart wondered what he could have done differently.

"I'm sorry, Doctor Gomez."

"Don't be," she said. There were tears in her eyes, but a small smile hid in her lips. "Keshav was right. Oh, and Stuart?" she said.

"Yes?"

"This constant use of Doctor feels terribly formal. You can call me Harper."

Chapter 17

I have read a lot of travel blogs, but not a single one that started with something like this: today I witnessed a demigod fall in battle to two others. I grabbed the staff of one of them and shot fire at it until it flew away in the sky. I punched a different demigod in the junk, and seconds later, he was burnt to a cinder.

There were blogs like that out there but they are full of stories of chem-trails, mind-controlling fluoride, conspiracies of aliens, and inter-dimensional beings. Crazy people talk. Is that what I've become? A crazy person?

That word no longer seems particularly relevant. Everything since I got to Argentina has been crazy, and that's especially true these last few days. Hmm. I can't really say days. It's always the same here, that purple sky. Truth is, I have no idea how long we've been down here. We've slept, walked, eaten, fought, swum, walked again, and yet it could be two days or ten. When I think about the people we left on the ship, I worry. But their fate seems far away not connected to me, to us. Like when you hear a flood in Bangladesh just killed a million people. It's sad but not on a personal level.

I threw away the staff of Ra after using it to drive away our enemy. I felt dirty, sick from using it. But Keshav has it now. He argued—not wrongly—that it was better to have it and not need it than the other way around. Many are the perils of this land, and we are otherwise unarmed.

After the battle, we were all tired, sick, and in shock, but it wasn't exactly the kind of place you hang around. We left, walking slowly. With the wandering boots on, we could inherently find the way. The forest grew thicker around us, and we all felt the eyes of unseen beasts on us. We could here birds talking, creatures growling, things scurrying in the underbrush. We stayed on the path, though, and nothing confronted us.

There was some thought of going back. The aspects of Ra left their ship. But somehow that made it all seem so meaningless. We must reach Graben. What will happen there is anyone's guess. But they must know we are no threat. Hell, we're not even knowledgeable enough to be pawns.

Keshav and I talked about it on the walk. We're not entirely sure we're on the right side. Or that there is a right side. The agents of Ra, well they did lead a golem army against Selvage, but those golems weren't really alive. They did kill Nala and drove away Ek Chuaj. But only after each attacked them.

I wish I knew more about Ra. Not that our myths would be super helpful knowing about Omphalos. But is he like Zeus— blustery and hot-tempered but a dependable guy? Or is he like Odin—a sinister god, a plotting Machiavellian dude?

I just re-read my last paragraph. Maybe I am going crazy, if these are my thoughts.

We are camped out now by a small stream. Even in the light, it was easy to go to sleep. I have first watch, and I'm about ready to crash myself.

But I'm worried. Despite being sunk, my camera still works. Good old Sony, plus that waterproof bag was worth the money. I checked it just now, before I started writing this. Obviously my journal is dry too, as are my extra batteries, and memory cards. Took a picture of the purple sky and blue brook. Put on a macro lens and took pictures of some orange flowers.

But not once today—not when being chased by bird-headed men across the sea, not when confronted by them, not when a striped god with a scorpion tail who accepts offers of chocolate, and not even when I had a staff that shot fire did I even think to take a picture. My camera is—was—my voice. My Self. When I don't even think to use it, what does that mean about me?

Chapter 18

It wasn't the next day in any way other than perhaps euphemistically, but after everyone had rested, the four of them continued their journey. Stuart had some dried mushroom meat in his backpack, and though it wasn't the tastiest of food, it settled their hunger pangs, and tasted better than it sounded. As they walked, they kept an eye out for the aspect of Ra to return.

Their wandering boots moved more forcefully, more confidently in a westerly direction, and they followed them hoping it would pay off. Keshav and Baruna walked in the front and Stuart found himself walking next to Doctor Gomez. Harper, he corrected himself. It was easy not to mention what had happened, easy to let it go. But with death so close, there was no reason to be overly cautious. Besides, he could hear her crying.

"Harper," he said. It felt strange to call her by her first name again. She didn't move her head, but her eyes shifted and met his. "I am sorry about yesterday."

She shook her head. "I have really bad luck with men. Two in one month are gone."

"Sounds more like their bad luck," Stuart said.

She was taken aback for a moment. "Of course," she said. "I didn't mean to imply otherwise. Anyway, Nala wasn't right for me. It just turns out that's what I like."

"I imagine you've never been hit on by a god before," Stuart said.

"Oh, I don't know. Every fit young man seems to think he's some kind of god."

Stuart smiled, but had nothing to say to that.

"That's the problem with being an attractive woman," Harper continued. "You can get anybody you want, except who you want."

"My heart bleeds," Stuart said.

"That sounded awful, didn't it? Forgive me. These past few days have been pretty rough."

Stuart could sympathize. She had lost more than any of them. The thought of Dean Maxwell's sudden end still left him cold. He wondered how much easier this would have been if Maxwell was still alive. He'd had guns, wilderness survival skills, and would have been a leader to them all.

"Still," he said. "You're kind of living the paleontologist's dream right?"

She frowned. "There's a thin line between a dream and a nightmare. I'd have been happy looking at seals and penguins again."

"Oi, you lot," Keshav said. "Look at this."

This was in fact a walled city. The stone walls were made of boulders, stacked up like marbles. They stretched through the forest, one lined up next to another, reaching ten meters high. The rocks had been treated, and some sparkled, others were clear, and entire sections were covered in moss and lichen. There was a uniformity to the differences, but to Stuart, it was like looking at a painting too closely to see the picture.

"It's beautiful," Doctor Harper Gomez said.

The stone city was part of the natural landscape. It had been created, of course. But there had not been the accompanying felling of trees, moving of earth, destruction of habitats that marked upper crust cities. This was the impression the city gave, though in truth, the four had only seen the outer wall.

Mindful of his pre-sleep thoughts, Stuart reached into his backpack, and removed his camera from the container. He wished again for his tripod, but even if he had it, there wasn't time. He snapped a few pictures of the wall, but without context it looked like bubbles, or strange grapes.

An idea struck him. "Harper, come here."

"You've still got your camera?" she asked.

"Uh, yeah," he said.

"It works? My watch doesn't work down here. How does your camera?"

"No idea," Stuart said. "But if time doesn't exist, perhaps that's why instruments that measure it don't work. Pictures work because they're capturing things that do exist."

"That sort of makes sense," Harper admitted. "In a weird kind of way. Wait, don't you have a clock on your camera?" The star pattern on her shirt and trousers disappeared momentarily, leaving her wearing clothes so dark they were almost hard to see.

"It's been flashing *12:00* since we got here," Stuart said. "That's partly what led me to my theory. The rest of the camera works. In fact, here, let's take a selfie."

"I don't want to," she said. "I look terrible."

"Oh come on," he said.

She sighed and stepped next to him.

Stuart captured half-a-dozen shots, with the round stone walls behind them. "We look good together," he told her.

"Look, you're not such a bad kid. But I'm an adult woman. I know what I want."

"I'm twenty-three. That's hardly a kid."

She smiled a little wistfully. "I probably would have said that too. I forget how that age felt. Like you're grown-up, but really only a few years removed from high school."

"High school was five years ago!" Stuart objected.

That bittersweet smile again. "Exactly. Five years doesn't sound that long to me."

"You're not exactly an old crone," Stuart said.

"I know. But I'm old enough. I want a family, Stuart. And a husband who's there for me. And babies. A family."

Her interest in Nala and Maxwell made much more sense to Stuart. Even if she'd known they weren't the exact right match, they at least fit the provider role.

"Hey, are you lot coming or not?" Keshav asked. He sensed the tone of their conversation, and he grew more somber. "Sorry, hope I'm not interrupting anything."

"Nothing at all," Harper said.

"See any sign of anyone?" Stuart asked as they caught up with the honeymooners.

Keshav shook his head.

"I have a strange feeling about this city," Baruna said. "Not just the architecture, but I feel like we're being watched."

"We probably are," Harper said. "The dwellers of Graben are supposed to be even more developed than Selvage and Omphalos."

"Well, are they going to invite us in?" Stuart asked.

"I suggest we look for a gate or a door," Keshav said.

At that moment, they all froze as a low growl sounded from behind them. It was a menacing, primal sound. Stuart recognized it immediately.

"Run!" he said. "It's the death beast," he said. Already he was scanning the city wall, looking for an entrance or a guard or any help.

The others did not panic. Well, they hadn't seen it before; Stuart was hardly surprised.

"Stuart," Keshav said. His voice was so calm. "Get behind me." Harper and Baruna had both already done so.

Stuart felt fear boiling within him and almost ignored the man. Then he realized what the staff Keshav held meant.

The "beast of death and destruction" burst from some trees to their right. It loped at them, huge mouth full of razor sharp teeth. In two steps, it had gained half the distance to them.

In three steps, it was a pile of ash. Stuart sighed heavily, fear at last relinquishing its cold grip on his heart. Baruna and Harper whooped in relief and the former gave Keshav a big kiss.

Keshav, though, shook his head, as if to clear it. "That much power. It doesn't feel right." "It's a weapon of the gods," Stuart said. "It's not meant for the likes of you and me."

"I understand why you abandoned it yesterday," Keshav said. "And yet I must keep it. Without the staff of Ra, we would all be dead now."

Stuart knew that for a fact. His attempt to run away had been sheer, blind panic.

"It might come in handy in Graben too," he said.

Keshav laughed. "I'm sure they've got toys of their own."

***

There were no toys in Graben. When at last they found an actual gate, even with their boots, a long weary walk from the site of the Andrewsarchus attack, they knocked and shouted. When no one came, Keshav used the staff to blast their way in.

They found an empty city. It was colossal and sprawling, far more like an upper Earth city than Selvage had been. Of human, or humanoid, inhabitants there were none. Through a tunnel and onto a street. It was circular and seemed to stretch around the entire city.

There were houses here, and shops, and immense buildings all made of the same bubble shaped boulders that the wall was constructed from. All had empty, vacant black windows and vacant black doors yawning with open, hollow mouths. And yet the city of Graben was not filled with an oppressive silence.

There was sound. Water trickled from somewhere unseen. Clicking and shuffling noises too.

"Hello," Stuart called, cupping his hands to his mouth to amplify his voice. His head tilted up as he scanned the upper stories of the buildings around them. "Is anyone here?"

"Quiet!" Harper Gomez hissed. "Obviously no one is here. Don't bring attention to us."

"If no one is here?" Stuart began but he let it drop. It was clear what she meant.

"Do you remember?" Baruna said. "Acan said they hadn't heard from Graben for a long time. Do you suppose everyone, I don't know, died? Or fell asleep?"

"Or left?" Stuart added.

"Or never was here in the first place," Keshav pointed out. "We only have what Acan told us. He might have had reason to mislead us."

"Why?" Harper asked.

"If we knew that, we'd be a lot better off. I can't even guess though, can I?"

"It's frustrating. Time is running out. We have no idea if those on the ship are even still alive. But they are counting on us," Harper said. "We can't afford to just dick around."

"We should at least explore the city," Stuart said. "I mean, we're here."

Keshav nodded. "I agree. But we stay together. I don't want to have to use this staff again, but I will if means it protects us."

They set forth into the forgotten city of Graben. The scale of the city was massive. Not mega on the scale of a modern metropolis certainly, but for a walled city it was bigger by far than medieval cities in the UK. Perhaps a million people could comfortably fit in the city, and they found not only fresh springs but rooftop gardens still growing carrots, chili, sweet potatoes, and tomatoes. The crops were wild and growing haphazardly, but still there were vegetables at hand. Soon after, they discovered subterranean mushroom caverns, with carefully labeled (though written in a language none could read) signs above different beds. These they left alone, content with the relative reassurance of the veggies.

The road they'd come in on was circular, and it accompanied the wall as it wrapped around the city. There were portions of the city that were not parks but rather patches of forest that had been built around. Meadows usually found only on isolated mountains were placed in the middle of the city, and they bloomed with colorful wildflowers. Lone oak and banyan trees rose mightily, alone like sentries, but in the middle of the road, or even sometimes within buildings.

The buildings were empty, not just of people but also of furniture, food, utensils, and anything else that might indicate people having ever lived there. Most were covered in dust, but there were no cobwebs or signs of insect life. The clicking, shuffling sounds they'd noticed upon first arriving continued to sound at different times, but they could never pinpoint the source.

Throughout their explorations, Keshav always went first, staff at hand. They set off, by mutual assent, heading deeper into the city. Graben seemed to have been built on a radial like grid, with several alleys and streets serving as spokes, connecting to the circular roads that popped up every so often. It was a logical system, and it made it easy to explore. They found more empty buildings, more meadows, more lone trees, more wild gardens; more nothing, in other words.

They had been snacking on pilfered vegetables, but at last it was suggested and agreed that they stop to cook some food. Now deep in the city, close to the center, they collected fallen oak limbs, and started a small cooking fire with the staff. The roasted sweet potatoes and chilies were a treat after so many meals of dried mushrooms, and the fresh stream water tasted like chilled white wine.

The insides of the round bubble houses were soft enough to sleep on. There they found rest, all of them save a rotating guard.

Each of them dreamed pleasant thoughts that night, and all woke up refreshed. Although no one on sentry duty could remember seeing anything at all, in the morning they all saw them.

Footprints in the dust.

Chapter 19

Baruna, who had been last on guard duty, buried her face in her hands. "I didn't see anything, I swear."
Keshav backed her up. "They could have been here before we came in," he suggested.

Stuart looked at the prints carefully. They hadn't been there before, as did Keshav himself. They ringed the exact area they'd been sleeping in.

The prints were not from an animal. No clawed beast had stalked them in their sleep. That, at least, was a relief. Nor were they entirely human, which is where the relief abruptly ended in favor of severe worry. Stuart looked more closely, kneeling in the dust as he stared.

There were five toes, but they were too uniform and too blocky to be human. It almost looked like someone was wearing a human shaped shoe, constructed in a factory somewhere.

"What do you think?" Harper asked. She hadn't moved from her bed.

"Killer robots?" Stuart suggested. "I have no idea. Apparently Graben isn't as empty as it looks."

Unsettled, they gathered their belongings, and prepared to plunge once more into the depleted city, not stopping to eat breakfast. After so long walking, there was no soreness in their calves or thighs, no blisters on feet or toes. There was not even a need to stretch, although Baruna still did at meals, and before sleeping. The wandering boots were incredibly useful, but their muscles had adapted to walking all day as well. Even though, of course, there weren't any days at all.

After some more exploration, some more foraging; this time Harper found orange red bell peppers thrice as large as any they'd ever seen. They had discovered the center of the city. It was obviously so, for a large square with no trees, no buildings, stretched before them. Most of the enormous space was filled with a sunken amphitheater, half-a-meter deep, and filled with chairs. It was a boundless stadium. *U2* or *The Rolling Stones* could have played there and not sold all their tickets.

But there was no stage, no screen, no obvious center of attention for that multitude of seats.

"Curious and curiouser," Harper murmured.

"Another place I thought about for our honeymoon," Baruna murmured, "was the Canary Islands."

Keshav wagged his head at her. "They don't have this there, I bet," he said. "Can't find a proper abandoned city like this just anywhere."

"No, they're too full up with beautiful beaches and buffets," she said, but now she was laughing.

Harper looked up into the sky. "At first I thought it was good that we didn't see that Ra creature again. But now I wonder if it didn't follow us."

"Why would he watch us sleep?" Keshav asked.

She shrugged. "There's more here going on. Didn't he say he meant no harm?"

"I don't know what's worse," added Baruna. "Him following us, and watching us, or him going home and telling daddy about us."

"Quiet," Stuart said. They looked at him, surprised at the harshness of his tone. He held his index finger up, listening.

"Don't you hear that?" he said, voice half-a-whisper.

The shuffling and clicking noises were all around them now. Thuds were audible too.

"Where is it coming from?" Harper asked. Keshav lowered his staff, his eyebrows bristling.

Stuart started laughing. "It's elementary."

He ignored the concern in the eyes of the others. "Rule out the impossible, and whatever's left, however improbable, is the answer, right?"

"I think that's heavily paraphrased," Keshav said.

"Whatever. Here's the thing. This isn't improbable nineteenth century London. It's as Doctor Gomez said. We're in Wonderland."

"I didn't exactly say that," Harper protested.

Stuart was not listening. He held both of his hands up in the air, the gesture of an Old Testament prophet. "Show yourself," he commanded.

Nothing happened. The empty square remained empty.

"Ah, hell," he said. It had been a crazy thought.

Keshav was at his side. "You feeling all right, mate? You look a little ill."

Stuart glanced at Keshav, at the Staff of Ra clutched in his hand.

"Do me a favor?" he asked. "Let's all do it."

"The whole prophet thing?"

"Bear with me," Stuart said.

"I know you North Americans like to make arses of yourself. It's not as easy for us. The British are reserved, you know."

"Please," Stuart said. "It probably won't work. But I need to know. Can we all try it?"

"Show yourself," Stuart and Baruna and Harper said, more or less in unison. Keshav followed a beat later.

"Ghost of Graben!" he boomed theatrically. "Reveal thyself."

Despite his suspicions, Stuart almost fell over as, instantly, a thousand thousand forms materialized before them.

* * *

The custodians of the city were not ghosts. The creatures that materialized around them were golems, and they seemed to obey or at least acknowledge the humans. These golems were far different from the ones that had attacked Selvage and Omphalos. Those had been creatures of war, harsh and angular, filled with stony bellicosity.

These were gentle giants; creatures of crumbling clay, of wood and moss, of smooth marble and tranquil spirits. They were crudely humanoid, varying sizes, but most around two to three meters tall. Each one looked different; each one appeared to have been hand crafted. Some had craggy wooden bodies and mossy hair. Others were polished and smooth men of marble.

He thought of them as men, though they were in fact sexless, or at least lacking external genitalia. Their crude feet would certainly explain the prints in the dust they had found as well. Looking at them all, Stuart changed his initial estimation. There were probably not thousands of thousands of them. That had been panic and surprise talking. But there were, he'd guess, something like four or five hundred.

They also, apparently, could turn invisible at will. They did not speak, not in a language that any of them could understand. When Keshav spoke simple commands, they obeyed.

"Vanish," he said and without any noticeable movement on their parts, they slipped out of sight.

"Spooky," Harper said, but her voice was full of excitement.

"Show yourself!" Keshav ordered. The golems reappeared. Keshav chuckled. "What else can we make them do?"

"Leave them be," Baruna said.

"She might be right," Stuart added. "Maybe best not to meddle with powers we don't understand."

"Ask them about here," Harper said. "Try to learn where we are."

Stuart removed his camera from the backpack and case, and surreptitiously took a couple of photos. He didn't think they would mind, or even notice, but best not to take chances. In the end, he took three great shots. The first was of a wood golem, his body made of redwood with clovers growing though different spots along his arms and legs. The second was a squat clay golem, whose flesh looked wet and moldable. Though few of the golems showed emotion, or even had faces capable of expressing motion, something about this clay fellow's face looked like he was smiling. The third photo was of Keshav, and he had his staff up high as he commanded the golems to explain where they were. You could see Keshav's mischievous grin, and the delight in his eyes, as the strange creatures scrambled to understand him.

It took some doing. Obedient though they were, the golems did not comprehend complex commands. At last a rocky golem seemed to understand, and the four of them were seated in the vast stadium. The rock golem, who was made mostly of grey slate, but had jags of quartz throughout his legs and arms, left them.

"What do we do now?" Harper wondered.

"It could be worse," Stuart said. "We could be watching Twilight."

Keshav laughed, but Baruna did not, and Stuart suddenly felt bad. He hadn't meant to bag on someone's favorite film.

"Or, you know, any major Hollywood movie. They're all trash, right?"

He was saved by the return of the golem. It moved smoothly, the rocks in its body working as well as skin, joints, and ligaments. In its hands were five balls of something dark and resin-y.

"Eh? What's this?" Keshav asked. The golem mimed putting a ball in its mouth.

"He wants us to eat them," Harper said, mouth puckered in anticipatory disgust.

Stuart accepted one. It was round, viscous, and made of grainy brown pellets. He sniffed at it dubiously, hoping for a chocolate scent. No such luck. It smelled of loam and earth.

"It can't be any worse than *Phan Pyut*," Keshav said. He dropped the ball into his mouth.

His face scrunched up instantly. "It's worse, it's worse," he said, barely able to enunciate his mouth was so full.

"What's *Phan Pyut*?" Harper asked.

"Potatoes," Baruna said. "Rotten potatoes, with liquid oozing out."

"What? Why?"

Stuart knew the longer he held his ball, the harder it would be. Pretending very hard that it was a truffle, he dropped it into his mouth. It actually wasn't that bad, for all that it tasted like bitter mud.

He was dimly aware of the others swallowing their portions, and then everything got fuzzy. His stomach heated up, and his head was wrapped in cotton. For a moment, he felt certain he was still in Manitoba. Was it the Jazz festival? Music of some sort sounded in his head.

And then he was, blissfully, nowhere at all. All around him was an absence that his mind wanted to call blackness, but he recognized as void. It was here that the act of pure existence filled him. It lasted less than a second. It lasted for all of eternity. Gradually he became aware of the others. They were there with him, though how he knew he did not know.

"I'm not being funny," Keshav said. "But I've never tripped balls like this."

"You're not tripping," Stuart said. "I'm really here. We all are."

"Why are we here?" Harper asked. "What does this have to do with the amphitheater?"

"I wasn't expecting Bollywood, but this is strange," Baruna added.

At her words, the void around them filled. Stuart smelled curry and onions, hear car horns and bells. He felt surrounded by a thousand people. Ahead of him, just barely visible, was the Taj Mahal.

"I don't believe it," Keshav said. "We're in Agra."

"We all can see it?" Harper said. Her voice was quick and high with excitement. "Don't you realize what this means?"

The Taj disappeared, along with the rest of India. White and sterile walls replaced them. Scientists looking into beakers and making notes filled the room.

"Come on, Harper," Stuart groaned. "Even your imagination is boring."

He thought for a moment, and the scientists turned into chimps; shrinking down until they were in clothes far too large for them.

"This is their entertainment," Harper Gomez said, completely undeterred by the monkey madness. "They achieved communal storytelling. The size of the stadium. It's an art from we can barely comprehend."

"We have something close to virtual reality," Stuart said. An image of a shady hacker straight out of *Neuromancer* appeared.

"Yes, only it's not that close. And that's only for one. That's the genius of this. It connects our consciousness in ways that words never could. Reality was never meant to experienced solo."

The hacker grimaced and collapsed, a hole in his jacket started smoking.

"You lot mind tampering it down for a bit?" Keshav asked. "I'd love to take my lady to the Maldives after all."

They both attempted to stop thinking. For several glorious moments, they were on a golden beach ringed by turquoise water. Dolphins leapt from the sea as the sand crunched under their bare feet. Without blinking, they were all SCUBA diving, accompanied by orange, blue, yellow, and green fish of all sizes.

All of those fish made Stuart a little hungry, and without realizing, they were in a sushi restaurant in Japan.

This went on for some time. Together they told stories, communal dreamers in a reality so fragile that a mere thought would change it forever until, at last, the effect of the spheres they had eaten faded.

They slowly regained access to their own stiff and confining bodies. The golems brought them food and fresh water. As they were eating, perhaps the strangest thing of the entire day happened.

Night fell.

Chapter 20

"It's dark," Stuart said. "I didn't even know that was possible."

"Is it because we're in the city? Or was it coming already?" Keshav asked.

"Or something to do with our afternoon's entertainment," Harper mused. "We just don't know. Regardless, I rather like it. I didn't know how much I missed the dark."

"Here's another question," Stuart said. "Is it going to be light again in a few hours or will it stay dark for as long as it was light?"

"Fair point," Keshav said. "I agree with Harper though. I kind of enjoy it not being all purpley all the time."

A wood golem with a mossy green Mohawk stood by them, much like a bodyguard. The others left; either by turning invisible or leaving, or perhaps both.

"That doesn't look good," Stuart said.

"Well, there are a thousand reasons why they would all leave. We can only guess," Harper said.

"I would like to hole up," Stuart said. "Just to be on the safe side. I sure don't feel tired though."

"I need to walk," Harper said. "My body is stiff from sitting in one position for too long."

"Actually, that sounds nice. Mind if I come?" Stuart asked. When she shook her head, he asked the other two. They declined, citing exhaustion, and he realized they had not had any alone time since the ship. "Ah," he said. "We'll take a nice long walk then."

Baruna looked moderately embarrassed, but Keshav simply smiled in gratitude. The Mohawked golem stayed with the couple as they found shelter for the night.

***

And so it was that Stuart Holmes and Harper Gomez found themselves walking through the city. It was dark, but still light enough to see. For the most part they didn't speak.

They walked up a pair of stairs carved into the stone. At last they reached a path along the top of the wall. It was wide and seemed to have been made for pleasure walks more than defense. Scattered wild flowers grew in bunches, and there were plenty of benches to relax all along the way. The views in the day must have been special, but now their high vantage point served to illustrate only how very surrounded by darkness they were. Stuart pulled out his camera and adjusted the light balance, but there was no shot to be taken, and he put the camera back in.

They walked along the pathway, counting the benches so they'd know how to get back.

"You know," Stuart said, after no one had spoken for some time. "This city is nice."

"It is," Harper agreed.

"I mean we've got food, water, servants. We're safe from the animals outside. We've even got entertainment."

She narrowed her eyes. "You're not suggesting what I think you're suggesting."

"You know, I think I am."

"Stuart," she whirled on him. "There's a dying man up there," she vaguely pointed up. "The captain is depending on us. What's more, there is an entire ship full of people who will die unless we help them."

"I know that!" Stuart said. "Of course I do. But first of all, we're lucky to still be alive. Those of us that are. We're twenty-first century travelers. We can't fight gods and beasts. Even if we could, even if we could get to the light source Acan told us about, it's been days now. It must have been. They're either dead already or help has come."

"We were the ones supposed to get help," she said.

"And we tried. No one can say we didn't. But time has passed. I mean, it could be months for all we know. Perhaps the ice has melted. Or someone found them. Cruise ships that size don't just disappear."

"That is rationalization and you know it," she said.

"Maybe it is," Stuart said with a sigh. "But the very plants here want to kill us. How are we supposed to survive against gods?"

"Maybe we're not supposed to survive, Stuart. But we have to *try*."

"Ah, hell," Stuart said. "I guess it would get boring here after a while. Besides, it's not like this place actually would defend us if Ra or Acan came looking for us. I think I'm just scared."

He sat down on a bench and put his head in his hands. The stone was still warm from the daylight.

She sat down next to him. "You know, I really had the wrong impression about you. I know men twice your age who still can't admit when they're wrong."

"I wasn't exactly wrong,' he said.

"Learn how to take a compliment, Stuart."

He did. They kissed, for a long time. At last they stopped, faces still close together.

"Last time I tried that, you almost slapped me," he said without thinking.

She gave a little laugh. "Last time you were being an asshole. This time you were being sweet."

Stuart didn't really understand that, so he kissed her again. He wanted to do more, to touch her body, and pull it close to him. He remained, however, overly-conscious of her boundaries. Instead of acting on instinct, he was over thinking. His hand gently went to her thigh.

She sensed his hesitation and pulled back. "It's kind of weird, isn't it?" she asked.

"Nah, I make out with hot doctors in all the abandoned cities I find."

She laughed at that. "That's probably technically true."

"It is. Unless you count Detroit."

"I'm actually from upper Michigan," she said. She held up her hand and pointed toward the top of her middle finger. "From here, Traverse City. Detroit is actually recovering quite nicely. It's got nothing on Graben."

No sooner had she finished talking than something big in the air descended onto them.

***

It was fuzzy, chittering, and battering at Stuart's head. Hairy antennae batted at them as more of the flying creatures descended upon them.

"Gah!" Harper screamed. "I hate moths!"

He realized she was right. They were moths, only they were bigger than eagles. In the dim light saw their orange bodies, wings grey, but flecked with yellow.

Instinct kicked in; Stuart punched at the animals. His fists ripped through wings and sent their bodies flying away, but always there were more. A moth wrapped itself around Doctor Gomez's head. He lurched forward, hands outstretched to grab it off her, but his face was covered by fuzzy wings. The hard nub of the moth's body pressed against his left ear. Stuart stumbled into Harper, and they both fell to the ground.

Harper caught herself, landing on her hands and knees.

Completely blind, Stuart fell hard and landed on his stomach. His forehead slammed into the stone ground. A bell rang loudly in his brain, and fragments of light exploded before his eyes. But the moth was squished by the blow, and its remains unwrapped from his head.

For a few moments, Stuart lay on the ground while the world spun around him. Above him, he could count at least eight giant moths in the air. There was no real defense against them, not unless he had a giant candle, or something. He wasn't sure if they were trying to kidnap or feed from them, but either way, the message was clear. *We're fucked.*

A giant candle. Or something. Inspiration hit. Stuart climbed unsteadily to his feet and pulled his backpack in front of him. Quickly he had his camera in his hands, and after a few seconds of fiddling, he had the right mode. The memory card he ejected and dropped into the waterproof bag.

"Hey moths," he called. "Say cheese, bitches."

He took their picture, flash turned on. The bright light stunned the moths, and Harper wriggled free. "Run back," Stuart said.

The moths rushed him as Harper slipped past him. Blood dripped down her forehead.

"Seven benches back," she said.

"I know. I'll catch up with you before you get there."

He flashed the camera again, and the moths singled out the bright light. They came all at once, all together. They came as animals, blindly responding to the flashing lights. They came at him in a mass, and feral fear pricked at Stuart's nerves.

I can't believe I'm going to do this. It was an easy choice though, easier than it should have been. Certainly easier than dying. Stuart pressed down on the shoot button and began taking a series of shots. Like a strobe light, it flashed at them. The oncoming moths stopped, paralyzed. The closest were a meter away from Stuart. He could have reached out and touched one on its fuzzy wing.

Stuart sighed, shaking his head slightly. *I'm going to regret this.* With the multi-shoot mode on, he threw the camera as far as he could. It sailed over the walls, and fell the far ground below. The entire time it flashed, strobe-lighting really, and it lit up the dark night sky.

The moths followed, instinct bringing them over the walls, and after the camera.

"I just threw away two thousand dollars of camera," he said quietly to no one in particular. "Not to mention the lens."

***

He did not catch Harper Gomez before the stairs. His eyes were night blind, and he made his way slowly along the top of the city wall. She was waiting for him at the top of the stairs. Good. He hadn't been sure if he'd come seven or eight benches, though his wandering boots had stopped at this juncture.

"What happened?" she asked. "Did you kill them?"

He shook his head. "Just distracted them. They could be back up here. Come on, let's go."

They made their way back to ground level. There were no visible lights in the city, but the streets were somewhat brighter than the black emptiness above.

Stuart felt worry churning in his stomach even after they got back to the ground. At any moment the moths could return. They walked briskly back to the square, where the Mohawked golem stood. It did not acknowledge their presence in any way.

"Should we warn it?" Harper asked.

"I don't know it would understand us," Stuart said. "Let's just get inside."

They entered the house next to the one taken by Baruna and Keshav. Though the kissing had been nice, both were too far too tired to do anything but fall asleep. With the golems about, they decided no one needed to remain sentry. Stuart had been lying down for less than a minute and was nearly asleep when Doctor Gomez's tired voice sounded in his ear.

"Stuart?"

"Yeah," he said.

"How did you get rid of them? The moths, I mean."

"There wasn't much to it," he said. He didn't want to talk about it. He didn't want to think about it. But there wasn't much point in hiding it from her. "I got them interested in the flash of my camera. There's a mode where it will take endless pictures, frame-by-frame. Once they were into that, I threw my camera off the wall."

"You what?" Harper didn't try to hide her shock. "That camera is your life."

"I would have said the same thing, not too long ago. I have learned, or am learning I suppose, that it's actually my life that's my life."

"Ha. Fair enough. Well, thank you. I owe you."

"You know what I miss more than my camera?" he said, uncomfortable with the open gratitude.

"What's that?" There was an edge in her question, and he realized she thought he was going to talk about sex.

"My toothbrush," he told her. "Or even just some toothpaste and my finger. It's hard to go sleep with a dirty mouth."

She laughed, a bit in relief he thought. Nonetheless, dirty-mouthed as the both of them were, they were both asleep quite quickly.

Outside the dark deepened, and then, much later, slowly began to brighten. When the four of them arose and met in front of the houses, (presumably) some hours later, it was bright as a summer dawn.

Though none of them yet suspected, it was to be their last day in Graben.

Chapter 21

They began with a fire and a hot breakfast of roasted potatoes and chilies. There weren't nearly as many golems out today, or at least they were not visible. Keshav and Baruna were shocked to hear of the moth attack the previous night. When Stuart somewhat reluctantly told them of how he had gotten rid of them, Keshav gasped.

"That was a brilliant camera. I'm sorry, mate."

Stuart shrugged. "I have two point-and-shoot backups and a GoPro. Only problem is, I left them." He trailed off, wondering if their ship was in fact still afloat. Had it been rescued already? Were there search parties looking for him? What were his parents thinking? Would his brother James and his sister Sophie still be going to classes at college? This was not the first time he'd had such thoughts, but never had home seemed so far off.

"I don't like moths," Keshav said, when the silence had become an entity unto itself. "And we know there are worse things out there." He took a bite out of a steaming sweet potato.

"They never came into the city," Harper said. "Fear of the golems, or whether, they just lost sight of us … I don't know."

"I don't like that it was a regular night either," Stuart said. "Long purple days are one thing, but at least they're consistent." He was sweating from eating half a green chili. "I wonder if different creatures only come out…"

The ground shook, as if from a distant earthquake.

"That can't be good," Keshav said. The golems seemed to be worried. Several of them shifted back and forth from visible to invisible.

"You know we're in trouble when the best case scenario is an earthquake," Harper Gomez said. They sat there for a few moments, all concentrating on the outside world.

The ground shook again.

"A herd of dinos?" Keshav asked.

"Who knows?" Stuart said. "It might not have anything to do with us."

Harper's expression showed how likely she thought *that* was. "Either way, we need to take shelter," she said.

They rose together. As they did so, the ground shook again. Baruna fell spinning to the ground, and a giant appeared in the distance

"Oh, hell," Harper said.

***

There was no mistaking the colossal figure before them. The Falcon Lord himself had come for them.

Ra was massive. As big as Godzilla, maybe. He was humanoid, with a human head and face. A blue and black feathered falcon headdress covered him from the top of his head to his shoulders. He wore the traditional *shendyt*, a white cotton skirt around his waist. His muscular chest was bare, along with his arms and legs below the knees. He barged through the city, knocking down buildings with tender ease.

"Can we get the golems to fight?" Stuart asked.

Keshav winced. "I don't see how."

None of the golems were even visible.

"What can we do?" Harper asked.

Ra drew closer, striding through the city. He bashed houses down, tore off rooftops, stomped flat gardens and wells. He must have known where they were, or seen them, because he strode directly at them.

"Run!" Keshav suggested. He and Baruna fled back into the house they had slept in.

Stuart remained a moment, staring as if compelled at the colossal creature. Harper tugged at his elbow.

"Come on," she said. "We can't stay here."

The towering god stopped for a moment. A massive voice sounded in the city, not necessarily from the god, but certainly because of the god.

"*HOLD.*"

The command was so palpable that Stuart felt his muscles tense up. He could not move at all; his legs were cramped and tight. Harper had frozen next to him. He could see her white teeth gritted in concentration.

With an immense effort of will, he rocked himself backward. "Let's get the hell outta here!"

He tore down the street. The plan, such as it was, involved drawing their terrible foe away from where Baruna and Keshav hid. Stuart had not, however, accounted for the speed of the giant god. Ra took one pounding step, and the ground shook. They kept their feet, but the god was suddenly only meters behind them.

"Hide!" Harper yelled. They dove into the nearest house. It was a two-story, basic marble house of the kind typically found in Graben.

"*COME OUT.*"

The voice filled the air around them. It did not sound entirely human, but only because no human voice could have such urgency, such richness, such command. The urge to comply was once again nearly overwhelming, and Stuart and Harper held each other's legs down. Stuart concentrated as hard as he could; he grew dizzy and lightheaded, and yet his legs carried him up and to the door.

"Don't!" Harper cried, but she was completely taken up with her own struggle.

At the entrance, the pressure lessened. Stuart grabbed the side of the door, and the cool marble helped ground him. He peeked out the door to see where their enemy had gone.

Ra's massive size was now a hindrance as he searched for them. Evidently the god realized this, for in a blink of an eye, he shrunk down to a mere six meters. He remained as tall a two-story building, but now he was on a more human scale. The god had not seen which house they had entered. With his great size and power, he punched through a building two houses away from them.

"What can we do?" Harper asked.

"You're the expert," he said. It came out harsher than he'd intended.

"I'm not an Egyptologist," she said. "Even if I were, that would mean recognizing him on a vase or coin, not knowing how to fight him."

Stuart peeked out the window again.

Ra's rampage continued. He did not look enraged or angry or even mildly annoyed. Instead, there was a look of reserved efficiency on his face; the look of a man taking the garbage out in the snow. He moved to the house one away from them.

"You know the myths though. What could fight him?"

"Unless you have a sixteen yard long serpent with a head of flint, I think we're boned."

"Do you suppose he'd let us surrender?" he asked.

"I suspect frying one of his aspects leaves that off the table."

"I guess we scramble and run. Each try to get somewhere different. Meet back at the gate we came in at."

"Okay," she said. Her tone said a lot: it was a shit plan, and guaranteed not to work, but there wasn't exactly time to refine it.

They fled down the stairs just as Ra reached their house. The god tore the roof off, and the two humans ran out, between his legs.

Quick as a snake, Ra twisted and grabbed Doctor Gomez.

"Nooo!" she called. Ra held her in his right hand. His left hand appeared over her and something red, an elongated crimson rain, shimmered down. Doctor Gomez vanished.

Stuart saw all that in one glance. He ran faster than he'd ever run before as the flight aspect of fight or flight took over. He ran into a building, out through the back, jumped through a garden, climbed a wall, dropped to another building, ran around to the front, found himself on a different street, ran back up toward the center of town, and then, just as a stitch hit him, he tripped over nothing at all.

He was going fast and fell with gawky lack of grace. His hands and knees scraped on the hard ground. His foot ached where it had hit something.

"Hey," a familiar voice whispered. It was Keshav.

Stuart picked himself up and limped over to the house where the saffron turbaned man hid. He was alone. He was crying.

"Did he?" Stuart asked.

Keshav nodded, miserably. "I didn't even try to fight back. I couldn't move, right? I didn't even think of the staff." He had it now, though, clutched tightly in his left hand.

"He took Harper too. It probably wouldn't have worked," Stuart added, nodding to the staff. "It's his weapon, right?"

"I should have tried. Besides, it worked on his aspects. I think we have maybe the only thing here to defend ourselves. Well, that and these three."

At his gesture, three golems shifted into the visible spectrum. One was the green haired Mohawk guard. The other two were clay golems, their bodies muddy greys and splotchy orange-reds.

"Is that what tripped me?" Stuart asked.

"Afraid so," Keshav said. "I asked 'em to grab you. I didn't expect that. Let me see your hands."

"It's nothing," Stuart said. His hands and knees were scraped and bleeding, but it was just road rash. He could shut away that pain until they were safe. "Are the golems still on our side?"

"I think so," Keshav said. "But I don't think they dare face what's out there."

"That limits their usefulness," Stuart said.

Keshav wiped sweat from his face. "Is it getting hot in here?"

It was like someone had turned the thermostat up twenty degrees, like they'd stepped into an oven. Keshav and Stuart turned to face each other.

"He's cooking us!" Keshav cried.

"We have to get out of here." Already the heat had doubled. Sweat poured down both of them.

They ran into the street. There was no sign of Ra, but all of the houses they could see were melting from great heat. The marble shaped material melted like candle wax. Burned wreckage spilled into the street. Out here the heat was better, but even their clothes felt too warm against their body. Both men were sweating profusely.

"Back to the center of the city," Keshav cried.

***

It did not take long to reach the central zone. Ra was there, waiting for them. The long feathers in his headdress were shriveling in the heat, but his body was completely unaffected.

Stuart and Keshav slowed and paced warily toward him. With a glance of acknowledgement, Stuart stepped to the right, while Keshav went left.

"*SURRENDER.*"

It was less difficult to deny now. Adrenaline and grief at losing Harper and Baruna made the siren call less dangerous. And yet it took fierce concentration. Stuart felt blood run down from his nose. It hit his mouth, all salt and copper.

"Oi, wanker!" Keshav's voice was loud and brave, but Stuart could hear how shit scared he was. "We've had enough of your shit, mate." The tall man held the staff steadily aimed at the enormous deity.

Ra did not so much as blink.

"Right then," Keshav shrugged and the staff sprang into power. Powerful energy shot into Ra.

It was so bright that both men had to close their eyes and look away. Jubilation and joy filled Stuart's heart as an odd noise sounded.

As the light died down and Stuart blinked back to vision, he realized the strange sound was laughter.

Ra laughed.

"*SIMPLETON. THOUGHT YOU TO SET FIRE TO THE SUN?*"

Ra gestured once. The staff in Keshav's hand exploded with the lethal force of several grenades.

Pieces of Keshav filled the square, but they were small chunks of flesh and bone. Nothing even recognizable as human.

"Where did we go wrong?" Stuart wondered aloud. He would have screamed, but at that moment, Ra grabbed him in his warm hands.

Chapter 22

Far away from Graben, to the west of Selvage, in the very center of the subterranean world, lay the city of Omphalos. As seen from afar, it resembled nothing so much as an enormous stone beehive. It squatted with ungainly bearing on a desert floor that stretched toward a distant mountain peak. The urban structure was indeed carved from a massive, mountain sized stone. On the inside, a warren of tunnels leading to various chambers of varying sizes made it livable. There were chambers for sleeping, for cooking, and for storage. The function, if not the design, was not dissimilar to that of a human apartment complex, or castle. Some of the inner rooms were massive, betraying the same predilection toward the grandiose that all of the gods had shown. The broad stone structure was an eyesore, made of stone and hubris, but within dwelt some of the most powerful and twisted gods in existence. Deities of death, goddesses of destruction, malevolent spirits, catastrophic brutes and ghastly miscreations all made a home in the city of Omphalos.

It was here that Ra brought them.

Chapter 23

Jesus. Where do I even start? I am in a cold stone cell somewhere that smells of mold and bones. Harper and Baruna are with me in nearby cells. Keshav is no more. It still makes me ill to think about it, and I haven't cried this much since my cat died when I was eight. But I'll say this. Keshav died like a hero. A secret geek who challenged a god to a battle? It's not much, but it's all I can cling to. I don't even worry if I'm a crazy person anymore. When the world is crazy, only the crazy would try to remain sane.

That sounded better in my head.

Almost as bad as him dying was that I had to tell Baruna. She was captured first, and it was up to me to inform her. I almost didn't. Couldn't.

Of course I had to. Just blurted it out, in the end. She didn't cry. She didn't make any sound at all. I haven't heard her cry yet. Where did we go wrong?

I never got a chance to write about it, but we found Graben. It was empty, except for some golems who seemed somewhat helpful, but also utterly useless. It was a pretty weird place. Architecture I couldn't even begin to describe. A city made of marbles, with parks, fields, and meadows. I think we could have stayed. I certainly didn't even feel the need to write. Not sure what that says about my "Self." I also lost my camera, which certainly mutes the Stuart who began this trip. I don't think that's who I am anymore.

Staying there was moot anyway. Ra came and took us. I guess he would have taken us all alive if we hadn't fought back. Who knows with gods?

I am not sure how long I've been here. They bring food twice a day, and it's good. Rice, lentils, noodles, onions and tomato sauce. The first actual cooked meal I've had here. I have my backpack and all my possessions as well. They're not too worried about us hurting them.

We are closer than ever to the disc of power, which is apparently in Ra's possession. But using it to go home seems pretty damned far-fetched right now. Five of us left for help, and now three of us remain, imprisoned. Some help we were.

I wonder about that isle of Mu. Or Lemuria or whatever. I remember Keshav's story about the lord of the volcanoes. Is that a different god than Ra? Surely the power of the sun is volcanic. Did he destroy his land? Was it to drive his own kind down here?

Why?

Keshav and I had wondered if we were on the right side. Well, Ra showed his true colors. We were fools to doubt Acan. He healed us, saved us, and sent us with protection to a city he believed would help us. Ra crushed that city and killed/captured us. I don't think I'll ever see him again, but if I do, I owe a big apology to Acan.

Earlier I thought we weren't knowledgeable enough even to be pawns. Now I wonder if that isn't the very definition of a pawn. I can barely see the board, but it's clear that moves are being made. I just don't know who's making them, or why.

Chapter 24

Not long after Stuart finished scribbling his blog entry, a young blonde woman came to them. She wore a blank expression and was nondescript other than her pointy, almost elven, ears.

Her name was Nakka, and she gave them hot water and towels to clean ("As is your custom," she said) and more food. The water smelled of iron, but after Stuart had wiped the grime and dried blood from his body, he felt worlds better. Their clothes remained spotless and stench-free, which was an even greater miracle. Not one of them, after all, had packed deodorant.

Nakka opened the metal door to their cells after and observed dispassionately as all three of the Upworlders hugged.

"It is from me you will learn something of the city," she said. "Follow me."

They hadn't taken more than three steps when she added: "And don't even think about trying to escape. I would take no joy in killing you three where you stand."

Stuart did not remember anything from being taken in Graben until waking up in the cell here. Thus, the long, smooth tunnels were something of a revelation. Such a wonder could not exist in the world above.

Harper likewise shook her head in amazement.

"I've seen cave homes in Cappadocia, but the scale here! I didn't dream of anything like this."

"Who lives here?" Stuart asked of Nakka.

"Many," she said. "Depending on how you define the word 'live.' Perhaps how you define 'who' as well." More than this she did not say.

They passed an open room where rusting automatons chopped vegetables, boiled water, and washed dishes.

"These are your chefs," Nakka said. "They cook for all the prisoners. Your dish is one that was popular in Lemuria."

"I know the separate ingredients," Stuart said. "But I've never had this before. They're pretty good cooks for robots."

"They are useless at all else," Nakka said. "Come on."

Harper followed. Baruna stared at the kitchen scene for a long moment, her face as blank as it had been since Stuart had told her. At last he grabbed her arm and gently led her after their guide.

They followed her through the warren. The tunnels between rooms were rounded and circular, and at times they shifted up. Some were at angles that would take magic or wings to get up. *Not a problem for most who live here, I guess,* Stuart thought. There were no windows to the outside, not where they were.

Selvage had felt earthy, at one with the world around it. Graben, even the ghost of it, had also felt somehow harmonious with nature. This place, for all of its novelty, felt *unnatural,* a constant sense of nails on chalkboard. He felt himself breathing heavily though he knew not why.

Other than the automatons, they saw no others on their level. Most of the rooms they passed were either empty or closed with locked doors. Nakka told them that they were close to the bottom of the city. So far down they were beneath the Earth. As the city rose, more important gods could be found. Ra himself dwelt in the uppermost chambers, the pointed top of the stone that resembled nothing so much as a pyramid.

"Let's go up now," Nakka said. They entered a stone cylinder. Nakka lifted her left hand carefully, and the chamber slowly rose.

"It's an elevator," Stuart said, surprised. It felt entirely too modern for this series of caves, even if it did appear to run on magic.

"You have something like this?" Nakka asked. "It has been long since I returned to the crust. Too long, perhaps."

Her long face grew even grimmer. "You need to know. What you're about to see. It's entertainment for us, but for you, it's the stuff of nightmares. Prepare yourselves, and know that no harm will come to you."

The center of the city, they soon saw, was a single chamber. Like a football stadium or hockey rink, but much larger and grander. There were rooms and seats surrounding a sunken rough stone floor. There was perhaps room for a thousand humans but currently only a few dozen sat in the stands. It was enough like the one at Graben that one clearly must have inspired the other.

Beneath them, the stone floored pit was covered with a translucent ceiling. And in the pit? It was far worse than mere nightmare. Stuart felt his heart beat faster as Doctor Gomez gasped audibly. Even stone-faced Baruna cringed back.

It was a full-on brawl. There were ugly one-eyed, one-armed, one-legged monsters riding eight-legged serpents. A three-headed giant made of iron stomped across the floor, the pulped remains of something in his hands. Winged felines as large as bobcats dripped venom from their fangs as they soared up toward the invisible ceiling. A group of twelve black furred yeti-like apes growled and rutted, ignoring the hundreds of eyes upon them, and the fighting of their companions. A skeleton with tattered wings fought against gibbering ghouls. A giant crow squared off against a fox with a hundred tails.

Worst of all was *she*; part-woman, part-snake, all evil. The air around her pulsated with disease, and creatures who approached her fell dead to the ground from her very aura. After staring at her for some seconds, Stuart vomited all over himself. There was no warning. One moment he felt fine, and the next spew covered his chest and legs.

"That's Ajatar," Nakka said. She gestured, and Stuart had warm, wet towels in his hands. "The Devil of the Woods, pernicious mother of plague and pestilence. Never has she fallen. Of all who have ever fought and bled here, she is the only one who ever joined voluntarily. It is a rare treat to see her here today, but do not stare too long at her."

"The others?" Harper asked. "The cats? The skeleton?"

"Creations of the assembled gods. They battle here, daily. Those with particularly useful or original creations receive high social status for some time."

"I see," Harper said, her voice subdued.

"Some of the monsters are new. Creativity is highly valued. But there is a status awarded to those who can win with a classic creature; a dragon, a Cyclops, a vampire. The battle is eternal. For thousands of Earth years, monsters have fought and died on the cold stone floor.

"Which one is Ra's?" Baruna asked. Her voice remained flat.

"Ra?" Nakka could not keep the scorn from her voice. "It is not fitting for him to participate. It would be as a father to children. Besides, he sent in a Sphinx once. It won, but the preceding riddle contest is remembered as the most boring of all fights."

A terrible feeling gripped Stuart. "Are you? Are we? Do you mean for us to fight here?"

"Perhaps," Nakka answered casually. "There is certainly some interest in how upper crusters would fare. You would be provided with modern weapons and armor from your world, of course. But you are a known quantity. We have killed humans by the millions, with sacrifice, disease, war, and ignorance. All qualities various gods have introduced into your world."

"Why are we here?" Harper asked.

Nakka shrugged. "I do merely as instructed."

"Is Ra coming for us?" Baruna asked. Her voice was harsh with disuse.

"No, I think not," Nakka said. "I know not why he came for you personally, but I suspect you will not see him again. The Falcon Lord has many duties."

She hesitated. "I hear he found you in the city of Graben." Her voice was low, confidential.

Stuart had to lower his ear to hear her over the sounds of the monster fight below. "I don't really want to talk about it. We lost a friend there."

"Aha. I understand human sentimentality. It makes no sense to grieve over what would have only been a few more decades anyway, but I understand that custom, and won't press anymore. Besides, considering the reputation of the guardians, you are lucky it wasn't more."

"Guardians?" Harper asked. "There were no guardians."

"You must have found a different city. The guardians of Graben are ferocious."

"We were in Graben," Stuart said. "Big city, amphitheater in the middle, lots of golems, weird shared hallucination balls."

Nakka stared at them. Her jaw actually hung open. "You survived the golems? I suppose it makes sense, though who would have guessed? No wonder Ra took an interest in you. I want to ask you."

Before she could continue, two figures approached them. Both were human-sized. One was dark-skinned and had a certain twinkle in his eyes. The other, also dark-skinned, had a faint fragrance about him. Neither looked familiar, though, either as people he had met, or familiar gods.

"Ah," Nakka said. "These are the ones who summoned you to the fighting pits."

"That will be all," said the twinkle-eyed god. "We will discuss with them the fight tomorrow. And then we shall return them to their cells."

Nakka hesitated. It was clear that her curiosity had been piqued.

"That will be all," the other one rumbled in a deep voice.

The tall woman bowed deeply and departed.

"Let us go down now," the first god said. They journeyed back to the stone elevator chamber in silence. Stuart still felt ill and frightened from the monsters they had seen. The five of them returned to the prison level, passed the automaton servants, and found themselves in front of their cells.

Before they could be reassigned to the cold dungeon cells, Stuart hugged the twinkle-eyed god.

"What are you doing?" There was as much amusement as outrage in his voice.

"I told myself if I ever saw you again, I'd apologize. We didn't trust you as much as we should have."

The air shimmered, and the men before him revealed themselves as Acan and Ek Chuaj. The former reverted to the same short and coarse hair, and broad nose. The latter looked bruised and somehow smaller, and his scorpion tale was nowhere to be seen, but it was undoubtedly he.

"You knew?" Acan asked.

"I hoped," Stuart said. "You had an air of mischief about you. And I didn't think that many gods would smell like chocolate."

"I don't understand," Harper said. "Why bring us up from prison only to bring us back down here?"

"It was important that you see the battle of the monsters," Acan said. "Very important. But I did not count on the presence of

Ajatar. Too much time in her presence would sicken you all, perhaps even kill you."

"You're here to rescue us?" Harper asked.

Acan sighed. "If it only it were that easy. No, the presence of the Falcon Lord here limits what I can do. I have made a deal with his subordinates, but it's the worst kind of compromise. It leaves us both unhappy. I'm afraid we're here to choose one of you and ensure you don't die when you fight in the pit tomorrow."

"What?" all them asked.

Acan held his hands up, placating. "It's the best arrangement we could reach. Ancient custom decrees that if you fight and win, you can all go free. Not even the Falcon Lord would interfere with that, though he would certainly forbid the deal from being made if he knew."

"You want us to fight a monster tomorrow. What if we lose?" Harper asked.

Acan frowned. "Then you all die. But that's what is going to happen anyway. This way you have a small chance of life."

Chapter 25

"Can the *balche* restore any who have died?" Baruna asked in a rush.

"It cannot resurrect the dead, child," Acan said sadly. "That power is beyond me."

"Then let me fight tomorrow. In the pit."

"No," cried Stuart and Harper together.

"The founder of the Sikh religion taught that men and women are equal," Baruna said defiantly. "There is a long history of female warriors and freedom fighters. From the sainted Mai Bhago the Guru's own bodyguard, to Jind Kaur, the Maharani, she who sowed the seeds of India's independence from Britain."

It was by far the most she had spoken since the death of Keshav. She also had a steel in her voice that Stuart had never suspected existed. He was instantly convinced of how important it was to her. He was also convinced it was a suicide mission.

"I can't let you," Stuart said. "I'll go."

Baruna whirled on him, her fists clenched. "It's not up to you. My father and brothers fought on the Pakistani border. I will fight tomorrow."

Harper pulled him away.

Baruna shifted her focus to Acan.

"I don't think there's any arguing with her on this," Harper said in a low voice.

"But she'll die," Stuart said.

"Maybe," Harper said. "Maybe not. It is her choice to make."

"Friends. It is dangerous for us to remain here. Our powers of camouflage work only on creatures of our own power. Many here would recognize us, and it would not be pleasant should we be discovered."

"I understand," Stuart said.

"I can give you *balche*," Acan said. "And Ek Chuaj will provide you with a weapon of your choice. We have also arranged for your fight to be against a relatively weak creature. Relatively," he added with emphasis. "It is still a terrible monster that will likely slay you."

"It sounds like there's a catch?" Stuart said. Something about Acan's tone made him feel nervous.

"I need to know what you saw in Graben," Acan said.

"Why? It wasn't what you expected, I can tell you that," Stuart said.

"Don't be so sure. Are the guardians still there?"

"I don't really want to talk about this now," Harper said. "Not here. In front of everyone."

By "everyone" she meant Baruna of course. But Acan was not to be put off.

"Are the defenses of the city still active? Did you see the darkness of night?"

"There were no defenses," Stuart said. "And yes it got dark there."

"That is not good enough. You are the first to enter the city in a long time. I must know more."

"Why?" Harper asked.

"It is not for you to question me. I owe you a life debt, true, but arranging the fight for you tomorrow could balance that."

Stuart could tell that Harper was just as frustrated as he. He'd always known Acan was capable of manipulation, but for it to be this apparent meant he must be desperate. And that little bit of power was like salve to the prisoners.

"We have to get rest and discuss," Stuart said. "If we survive, we will tell you more."

Acan was not pleased, but he made arrangements to meet them out of the city after the fight, should they survive. "Ra is gone now," he said in a low voice. "That is why we are moving so quickly. He wouldn't oppose custom, but he'll be mightily unhappy to learn his prisoners have escaped. Meet us and we will get you to freedom as quickly as possible."

The two gods left, leaving the humans in their cell. Acan had put them all into one room; it was cold, hard, and not exactly spacious, but it was nice to remain together.

Harper turned to Baruna. "What can we do to help you prepare?"

"I'm ready," Baruna said. "I've always known how to heal. But I don't have to hide it from him anymore. Now I'll see how I can hurt."

***

"Come on, Baruna!" Stuart yelled. He and Harper sat together, with watchdog Nakka, behind them. The stands this day were fuller, as perhaps two or three hundred other gods interested in the battle of upper crust human versus monster had gathered.

Baruna looked ready. She was clad in something very similar to chainmail that covered her from neck to knees. A string around her neck bespoke of a vial of *balche*. But her weapon?

"I was expecting her to have a scimitar of some sort," Stuart said to Harper.

She shook her head with worry. "She should have taken one of those laser pistols."

Stuart nodded his appreciation. "That's even better. Is it too late to change?"

A roar sounded, filling the large area.

"I guess that answers that," she said.

Baruna moved, holding her stick in her hand. It was a two-meter long branch, solidly thick with iron on each end. A quarterstaff was the technical name, but either way it was no more than a stout stick. Stuart couldn't guess why she had chosen that over a real weapon.

And then the monster appeared. Stuart recognized it instantly. It was smaller than an Andrewsarchus, smaller even than a modern day lion. But it was dense, massively built. Short legs held up the stocky body, and it had a short, bobbed tail. Two large, serrated canines extended from its mouth. They were at least eighteen centimeters long.

"Smilodon!" Harper whispered in dismay.

"A saber-tooth tiger. Oh shit," Stuart said. "She's dead." The beast roared a challenge. It was agile, quick, and it padded toward Baruna, with a hunter's grace.

"I can't look," Stuart said. He raised his hands before his eyes, but he could not look away from those long, deadly teeth.

A murmur went up from the assembled gods.

Baruna had first blood. As fast as the Smilodon was, the human woman had greater lateral quickness. And fast she was. Her body moved with grace and precision, as she slid behind the animal, and swung her club hard into its leg.

The Smilodon whimpered as its leg broke.

"She mentioned to me once that she could fight," Harper said. "I had no idea she meant something like this."

The saber-toothed cat whirled on her, great jaws opening wide. Those two long teeth glowed with potential violence. Baruna calmly smacked her staff down onto the creature's tongue. It bit down, tearing her weapon in two. She slipped behind it and whacked the cat's other rear leg with both ends of her stave. The leg shattered, with a bone-crunching sound that made Stuart wince for all that he cheered.

With its two rear legs done, Baruna made short work of the Smilodon. She sprang onto its massive back, clutching the ragged ends of her cudgel. The beast did not want her there and bucked once, but Baruna leaned forward, and held a broken stave in each hand. With a snarl, she shoved each pointed end into the animal's eyes. The fight and the life fled at once from the cat. Baruna jumped down, face passive. She was hardly even breathing hard.

The entire fight had taken less than three minutes.

Stuart was so shocked he could think of nothing to say. Beside him, Harper was beaming, just beaming.

"I thought she was going to die today," she confessed in a low voice. "I thought *we* were going to die today."

For most of the assembled gods, the fight was a disappointment, but Stuart and Harper gave her a standing ovation. Baruna was shuffled off as a tusked pig as large as a bear was brought in to face a creature seemingly made only of steam.

Stuart saw no more of that fight as he and Harper, trailed by Nakka, went to meet Baruna.

She seemed more alive, though still far from happy.

"Baruna! That was amazing," Harper said.

"I am so sorry I didn't trust you," Stuart said. "I would have been Smilodon dung."

Even Nakka added to the praise. "I did not know you upper worlders could fight so well."

"What kind of kung fu was that?" Stuart asked, who had watched his share of MMA fights and Shaolin movies.

Baruna frowned, unhappy at the attention, but unable to hide from it. "My father trained me in the science of weapons. Shastar Vidiya, we call it. It developed in the seventeenth century when we were under attack from both Muslims and Hindus."

"But when is the last time you fought somebody?" Harper asked.

"Every moment I am awake, Shastar Vidiya is always with me."

A loud crash reverberated throughout the city. There was a sound and a smell that defied description but made cold sweat appear on Stuart's palms.

"What was that?" Harper asked.

Nakka looked upward. Her expression was of one who unexpectedly bit into a lime.

"That is Ra. He has returned from the upper world."

Chapter 26

True to her word, Nakka led them out of Omphalos. She didn't speak much and hurriedly led them down to another level, one between their cells and the fighting arena. They emerged into the purple twilight. The smell of fresh air hit them with wondrous power. Even the harsh scent of the cracked desert around them was a relief after the tight quarters of Omphalos.

"Selvage is that way," Nakka said pointing to the east. "Follow the trail as best you can."

They said goodbye to Nakka, who in her own odd way had humanized Omphalos somewhat for Stuart, and began walking east. Before they had taken more than a few dozen steps, a rider appeared on the horizon.

They were quickly united with Acan, who came with four Selvagian megamoose.

"You survived," he cried. "I hoped, but did not know it would be so. Ride with me now, away from this damnable city."

Harper and Baruna each knew what they were doing, but Stuart had not ridden a horse since he was a child. It was difficult to even climb on these massive beasts, and their antlers, up close, were so big that it was hard to see how they kept their heads up. Fortunately the moose were quite tame, and the desert was flat and the ride was not too uncomfortable.

Baruna descended back into silence. Stuart wondered where she was, in her head. Back in the UK with Keshav? Or a little girl growing up on the Punjab? He shook his head. He was no grief counselor, and he could only guess at what it must be like for her. Harper rode next to her, on a particularly flatulent moose. Stuart and Acan were a couple of meters ahead of them. Though he knew it wouldn't help, Stuart glanced back at the monolithic Omphalos. Escape had seemed too easy, and he felt once more like events were happening too quickly.

Acan chuckled softly. "He's not coming after you. Not yet."

"We will be safe in Selvage, right?" Stuart asked. "How far is it?"

"How far is Selvage?" Acan asked. "Far. Ek Chuaj has returned to marshal our peoples. A long-awaited battle is almost upon us. But we are not returning all the way back to Selvage."

"We aren't?"

"Oh no. There's no need to go return there. We will clash with the armies of Ra at the Cinnamon Hills."

"We're not going to Selvage?" Selvage had been the only safe part of their trip since he'd left Argentina. "What is happening at these hills?"

"I mentioned this land to you once. The Cinnamon Hills are where light breaks through from the true surface. It is this we catch and spread throughout our realm, though it is faint, and the crystals in the earth give it a purple hue. It is also here that we charge our crystal armor. Here that the eye of Ra is at its most powerful. It is the nexus of our land. It is why war between Selvage and Omphalos exists. "

Seeing the worried look on Stuart's face, he added: "What's wrong? Once we defeat the Falcon Lord, you can return home."

"It's not that I don't want to, believe me," Stuart said. "I just am not sure we can defeat Ra. I mean, you saw those monsters they fight with. How could anyone have a chance against that?"

"Not all of those monsters are for war," Acan said. "Though they take their battles seriously, they don't quite have the same passion as they do for entertainment. It's easy to lose a war. Every immortal has lost more than we care to remember. But if you live forever, entertainment is of utmost importance."

"Okay, that aside. I mean, none of you can oppose Ra."

"This is true. But he rarely acts upon such matters himself. We would not act as we have if it were so hopeless."

That brought up something that had been bothering Stuart.

"How does it work? I mean, Ra is here. But is Thor? Zeus? Loki? Anansi?" He'd learned of the latter from a Neil Gaiman book. "What gods are real and what gods are not?"

Acan smiled, showing his teeth. "Apologies. I am not laughing at you. I forget how ignorant you mortals are. Lucky for you, it is a long ride to the Cinnamon Hills."

As they rode, Stuart learned that their enemy wasn't really the Egyptian god, Ra. More like, the Egyptian legend was a shadow cast by the real god. The same being's shadow had been interpreted as Zeus, as Shiva, as Haldi, as Xipe-Totec, as Cernunnos, as Amaterasu, as Nyarlathotep, and as a hundred other names that Stuart did not recognize. The more powerful the gods, the more incarnations they seemed to have. Acan himself, he said, was barely known outside of South America.

Not everyone on Lemuria, and here in the center of the world were, strictly speaking, gods at all. There were always those willing to follow those more powerful. The men who had ambushed Acan were just men, servants of Omphalos.

Stuart was not an expert on mythology. But there was one big god he felt like was conspicuous by his absence.

"So this Falcon Lord is the presence behind the myths of Zeus, Ra, and Shiva. But not Odin?" he asked.

Acan winked at him. "There's only one Odin, man."

"Where is he now?"

Acan shrugged. "The Gallows Lord goes where he pleases." He turned to face Stuart. "Now I need you to tell me more about Graben."

Stuart told him all there was to tell. The attack of the moths bored him. The threat of monstrous beasts did not warrant a comment. But when Stuart told him of discovering the invisible golems and the shared pleasure balls, Acan grew excited.

"They did not fight you? The golems."

"Of course not," Stuart said. The very idea was funny. "They helped us."

"I knew they would! I knew they must. But you told me you did not encounter the guardians."

"I didn't know that's what you meant."

"Ah yes. I constantly underestimate your ignorance." There was no malice in Acan's voice, only good cheer. "The guardians are the golems, of course. Created by the people of Graben."

"And who was that? We found no sign of any living people."

Acan pursed his lips. "If you haven't discovered that for yourself, I don't want to ruin the surprise."

They rode on in silence for some time.

***

The landscape gradually changed as they reached the Cinnamon Hills. Stuart blinked, unable to believe the landscape before him. They had seen a lot of new things at the center of the Earth, but nothing this truly beautiful.

Dark green forests grew over emerald green grass. Little wisps of fog drifted sluggishly through the thick forest leaves. This would have been striking enough, but there were thousands of conical brown hills rising across the gently rolling plain. Some were nestled together, others stretched out of the forests in solitude, but there were more than his mind could comprehend. With the purple sky above, it made him miss his camera for truly the first time. He would like to bring his sister here, he realized.

It's the most beautiful place I've ever seen, he realized. Up until now, The Pas in northern Manitoba had been his number one, but that was mere blue lakes and granite cliffs. These cinnamon brown hills, climbing out of the carpets of green, represented a splendid alien vista.

They waited there for a few moments, just before crossing a small stream on the edge of a forest. The women had fallen a little behind. Stuart's moose wandered over to a tree, and began stripping off the bark, chewing it. Stuart slipped off his moose and realized how sore his thighs were. He stretched and ambled down to the brook, where he splashed the dry desert dust off his face. Then he drank deeply from the stream. The water tasted of berries, moss, and everything nice. He drank until his stomach hurt.

When he looked up Acan was frowning. "They're almost here. But there is something close behind them."

Stuart stared back the way he came. Harper and Baruna had almost caught up. They were riding quickly now, too.

"I don't understand. What?"

"Get on your moose," Acan said. "Now." Never had his voice sounded more authoritative.

Stuart did not hesitate to obey. He found his moose, where it had stripped most of the bark of an elm tree. The women caught up with them just as Stuart ascended his mount. They did not pause, but carried right on through, splashing through the stream.

Acan caught up with them. "Ah!" he cried. "They sent the mokoi! Come, we are not far now."

As his moose lumbered forward, Stuart looked back and immediately wished he hadn't. He could see them now, in the air. They were only half-substantial, as though made of mist. They looked like big birds with heads similar to that of a condor. Needle-sharp fangs lined their mouths. Long wings carried their bodies, spanning three meters, like that of a bat or gargoyle. Long jellyfish tendrils hung from their bodies instead of limbs.

With an involuntary shudder, Stuart turned, and caught up with the others.

Acan galloped ahead, but as the forest closed in, they found themselves on a small game trail. It was wide enough for the megamoose to fit on, but they had to ride single file. Stuart fell back, putting his body between the two women, and the ghosts. He tried not to picture the vulture faced, ghost like mokoi catching up to them. Twice he thought he felt something on his neck, but it was only leaves.

Nonetheless, his skin broke out in goose bumps, and he felt his heart beating, all too quickly. There was no doubt from his body that the creatures were close. A slithering sound filled his ears. His mind filled with images of writhing maggots, worms crawling through eyeballs, and leeches swelling with yellow bile.

"Stuart!" Harper yelled.

He realized his moose had stopped, and his eyes were closed. All around him were the dreadful mokoi.

He felt drunk. His body wouldn't respond to his panicked mind, and his head awkwardly lolled back and forth. Tendrils dripped slime and mucus on him now, as the ghastly spirits descended upon him.

A shining blue disc came soaring at him. He wanted to duck but still had no control. It hit one of the mokoi, and sparks jumped as the creature dissolved in the air. It left nothing behind save for a patch of bad air that would put anyone who walked through it in the next month into a bad mood.

The other mokoi rose in the air. A high-pitched screeching indicated some sort of alarm on their part. The disc boomeranged in the air, and flew back to a dark hand.

It was Erinle, Acan's companion from Selvage. Behind him were three other Selvagians. They flung their blue discs together, and the missiles sailed over Baruna and Harper, flew just under some low tree branches, and then narrowly went over Stuart's head.

He could hear more sizzling, but control of his body was not yet his. Harper rode back to him, grabbing his moose by the antlers. It slowly prodded forward, apparently as affected by the wraiths as its human rider.

Stuart was only half-conscious as they rode past the warriors of Selvage. He was hallucinating—fever-dreaming—and only a very minimal participant in reality altogether. Images of other worlds mixed with graves and moldering bones. After a small while, however, he began to realize that trees were trees, his moose was a megamoose, and he was Stuart Holmes of Winnipeg, Manitoba. With those linguistic reassurances, he sighed deeply, and became human once more. Acan never did inform him how very close to death he had gotten.

Behind them, the last of the mokoi were killed or driven away by the plasma discs of the Selvagians. Ahead of them was the forward camp of the Selvagians. It was set high on one of the rounded brown hills and bathed in pure, golden sunlight that descended from the sky. The brightness of an April spring morning, rich and suffused with atmosphere, filled the area.

Acan meet them, already clad in crystal armor from the waist down. "Good," he said. "I hoped Erinle and the others could save you in time. Now we must prepare."

"Prepare?" Stuart asked. He still felt drugged. "For what?"

"For war!" Acan said, merrily. "The forces of Omphalos are closing in. Prepare yourselves!"

Chapter 27

We don't have long, and this is probably my last entry. In fact, I'm lucky to get this one, as I was just attacked by spirits who nearly drained my life away. Not much of a story there, apart from what I just said, so moving on.

We escaped Omphalos only because no one, deity or human, had counted on what a warrior Baruna is. She fought for our freedom, and she utterly destroyed a saber-toothed tiger. No one guessed she had it in her. I mean, she was like nothing I've ever seen. Apparently it was a side of her she was trying to leave behind. She didn't elaborate, but I got the sense that Keshav's family wasn't too keen on that practice. She used the word "old-fashioned." I spoke to her a few moments ago. Told her I was missing Keshav too, and she should feel free to talk to me if she ever needed to. No doubt Harper has done the same, but I think it helped her. She has been withdrawn—which is natural, of course. But I worry that with everything else going on she won't make the best decisions.

Everything else going on. A battle looms. I feel a little like Peter and Edmund must have before the White Witch's army came crashing down on them. This is for real now. There is good news. The crystal power armor that we saw our first time in Selvage? We get some of our own for this battle. It's still not super clear to me what we're fighting for. Surely it cannot be simply a patch of sunlight? I guess, on the other hand, we fight over patches of dirt, beds of oil, which gods to worship. It's sort of bleakly reassuring to know the gods aren't above scarcity battles.

I learned a little from Acan as we prepared. This is not the first time the two cities have fought. Selvage broke off from Omphalos not that long ago, as I gather; at least as how gods tell time. There have been battles since then, though whether two or ten, I cannot guess. He hinted that we unbalanced Ra when we killed one of his aspects. That was the reason he left his tower to claim us. Each time, it is for the right to share the sunlight areas, but also to use the disc of Ra. I think. How we got involved is still kind of weird. I feel like if I had time to stop and think about it, I could get some insight, but as it is, there is scarcely time to breathe.

I should be pumped. The armor should keep us safe, Acan says, but we are going to be fighting gods and monsters. I just feel tired. I mean, it's good to know that if we win we can go back home. But the upper world feels like it belongs to someone else now. Just thinking about that ship, which in all honesty I know must have sunk into the frozen sea not long after we left, makes me feel nervous.

I am not a religious man. Well, I guess I do believe in gods now, because, well, how could I not? But I don't subscribe to any of the major religions. And yet, I keep thinking about what Baruna said when we first got here. What if we all died—out there on the ice?

And this is just hell?

Chapter 28

The crystal armor fit with surprising comfort. On the outside it was all hard angles and jutting crystal nubs, but the inside felt as soft as velvet. Stuart was not sure if it was powered by magic or an unknown technology, but regardless, it felt like it weighed nothing. He could feel the armor respond to sunlight. It purred, like a pleased cat getting a back scratch. Nonetheless, Stuart felt somewhat ridiculous after putting on the helmet. A warrior he was not, and even with the armor and a borrowed laser pistol, he feared the upcoming battle. It seemed like such a pity. The youngest person here, by far in most cases, he felt far too old for this hostility.

From the top of their sun-drenched hill, the view remained stunning. But the verdant forests, for all their beauty, hid the oncoming army. Several warriors of Selvage were stationed at the bottom of the hill in order to better see. In armor, nearly everyone looked the same. He could only tell Baruna and Harper apart from the green swirls on their armor. He had the same markings on his armor.

It took only a few moments to find Acan. He was engaged with Erinle and Ninkasi, who was leading the forces of Selvage.

"Can I speak to you for a moment?" Stuart asked.

Acan visibly hid his irritation. "Omphalos is almost here. I must plan."

"It will only take a moment."

Acan excused himself and joined Stuart.

"It is okay to be nervous," he told the Canadian.

"What was Ra doing on the surface?" Stuart asked.

"You know about that, do you?"

"Yes. We heard in Omphalos."

"Of course. I do not know. He travels many astral planes, does the Falcon Lord. It is not for us to understand."

Stuart was no expert on psychology, but he knew an evasion when he heard one. He also suspected there was no point pressing.

"I am nervous. You're not wrong about that. We are fighting gods. Even in this armor, how can we hope to survive?"

"Now, Omphalos is a much bigger city than Selvage. They are the center of everything here. The denizens are more powerful as well. As such, they won't be leading the attack themselves. Their army will likely mostly be made of lesser creatures again. Engage them. Kill them. Leave the leaders to us."

"Lesser creatures like the Andrewsarchus or terror birds?" Stuart asked, voice rising.

"More terrible than that. But certainly not as terrible as the gods."

"What if they come after us?" Harper asked.

Acan tilted his head for a moment as he considered. "We marked your armor with green bands. We will try to protect you. Failing that? Run away. Live to fight another day."

"Are we going to ride on the megamoose?"

Acan shook his head. "Doughty though they are, they would die in the upcoming battle. And should we lose, we will need to them fresh to affect our getaway."

A shout went up from the guards at the bottom of the hill.

"Now I must go," Acan said. "Try not to die. You may be in for a surprise." He left Stuart and rejoined his companions.

Stuart glanced about for Harper and Baruna, but the forces of Selvage were flowing down the hill. Not knowing much about battle tactics, Stuart assumed the little he did know went out the window when dealing with forces that could fly and cast magic.

He took three steps down the hill, pistol clasped in his gloved hand, when the forces of Omphalos broke into sight.

***

The first thing he saw was giant ants. Most were black, but a few bright red ones marched as well; they were three meters long and two meters tall, with dusty and tattered skeleton warriors riding their backs. The ants were big enough that their mandibles could snap through the trees. They cleared the way for the rest of the army. Immediately behind the ants were floating desert ghouls. They bore the shape of emaciated humanoids; pale skinned, with dark clumps of hair, and cadaverous faces. Their arms were long, almost to the ground, and their hands ended in long sharp talons.

Stuart stopped, horrified by the sight before him. Already the first of the Selvagians were engaging the colossal ants. But now moving into view were six meter long centipedes with horned demonic faces and human arms at their front. Marching with them were shiny, sharp creatures that at Stuart's best guess were elementals made of glass. They carried no weapons as their entire bodies were razor sharp. Behind the elementals and centipede men were massive wolf spiders; two meters long, and with their long hairy legs, stood high off the ground. Over short distances, these aggressive hunters were some of the fastest creatures in the land. Marching warily next to the spiders were bestial, barking, furry cave men with huge heads, and wearing armor fashioned from cacti. Long dark needles and red flowers adorned their dark green breast plates and rounded helms.

In the sky overhead, vultures circled lazily. Had he looked closer, Stuart would have seen that instead of stomachs, the vultures had leech-like bellies which could suck all the blood from a human being in under a minute, leaving their body a withered, desiccated piled of bones and skin.

Such were the forces of Omphalos. Against them, a hundred demigods clad in crystal did not have a chance in hell. And yet the forces of Selvage charged forward. Time and time again, armor kept them safe. Stuart saw one fighter caught in the mighty mandibles of a red ant. It snapped close with boulder shattering force but did not separate the being in the armor. Instead, the warrior calmly raised their laser pistol and shot the ant through both eyes. The eyes burst like ripe papayas, and the skittering creature slumped to the ground.

Elsewhere Stuart saw a crystal-clad warrior hacked at by a pack of desert ghouls. A spider was eating some of the cactus-clad men that were its nominal allies. Glass elementals were a match for their crystal clad opponents in hand-on-hand, though they did not fare well against the laser blasts. One picked up a fallen gun and started firing at the warriors of Selvage. Men and women dodged and fell, cursing. Meanwhile, vulture bodies variously swooped and fell from the sky, contributing greatly to the hellish chaos.

Stuart was only halfway down the hill, but he was firmly in the vanguard. A centipede man tore through the two warriors in front of him and reared up. Though it had a humanoid face and arms, it could stand up almost to its very length. One of the hands carried a jagged sword as big as Stuart himself, and it came swinging at him.

Perhaps the armor would have protected him, but he did not want to take that chance. Stuart leapt back, almost falling over. The sword missed him by centimeters, and Stuart could feel himself sweating with fear. He raised his pistol at the monster, but the sword came whistling at him again.

The counterstroke was so fast he didn't even have time to react. He simply sat down reflexively, landing with a thump on his butt. Once again, the sword came uncomfortably close. The centipede man opened his human lips and emitted a terrifying bass chirping. He switched his grip, so that the sword would point downward, and then drove it down.

Stuart didn't even aim, simply pointed his pistol, and fired. Lasers shot out and, though none hit his monstrous foe, one caught the sword blade and dissolved it into shrapnel. The centipede man emitted another series of deep insect noises. He then dropped to the ground, going horizontal, and slithered the last meter toward Stuart.

A lucky shot took an arm off, but then there was a hand on his. The crystal armor protected him from injury and punctured the being's remaining hand, but the creature did not seem to feel pain. Stuart had the pistol squeezed from his hand. It leered at him. Up close, the demonic face of the man was terrifying. It didn't look human at all; from the horns on top of the head to the curved teeth in his lipless mouth, it was a face of diabolical woe.

The centipede man opened his jaws impossibly wide and lowered himself on Stuart.

A glowing disc tore his insectoid's head from his twitching body.

Stuart's body went limp from relief, but then the ichor and blood coated him as the centipede body fell onto his own. Cursing, he scrambled up with a distinct lack of grace and sought his benefactor. The disc looked like the one that Erinle had used earlier, but there was no one there.

Did that mean what he hoped it meant?

Stuart grabbed his pistol. The main battle had left him, had spread farther from the hill. The fighting was now almost twenty meters away. In the middle, the giant ants and their skeleton riders, along with the glass golems and centipede men, were giving ground to the fierce laser fire. On the right, the ghouls and spiders were winning, and there were scattered bodies clad in half-destroyed armor littering the ground. Most of the leech-vultures were dead or dying on the ground, though a few still circled expectantly over the battle.

On the right, the beastmen had moved as far away from the spiders as they could. They were fierce and canny, and low tech as they were, they were holding their own against the forces of Selvage. He blinked and looked again. Two of the crystal warriors had green bands. Readying his pistol, Stuart jogged over to find his friends.

* * *

The three of them briefly greeted each other, but there was too much to do. A giant red ant, blind and enraged, but not dead, stormed through both sides without caring overly much about whom it hurt. Finally, Baruna sent its smoldering corpse back to the ravaged earth. Sighing in relief, the three humans turned to face their next threat.

And then the bestial men began to drop dead. Untouched, unharmed; as though someone had unplugged them. Within moments, there were none left. All lay on the ground, still as a winter graveyard. A moment before he began to feel ill, Stuart's mind grasped the awful reality.

"What was her name?" he gasped. "The snake woman. The Devil of the Woods."

"Ajatar," Harper said. Her body slumped under her armor, and their foe still was not even visible.

Ajatar, the mother of plague, slithered into view. The trees beside her withered and died. The ground she covered would never again blossom. She was more awful than Stuart even remembered. He was not the only one to feel fear.

"Aieeee!" yelled a warrior of Selvage. "We must flee!" He turned and ran back up the cinnamon brown hill.

Stuart was about to follow him when Baruna stepped forward. The wave of nausea had grown stronger, and it took all of his concentration to even remain standing, but the woman from Wolverhampton slowly strode out to meet Ajatar.

"What are you doing?" Harper cried.

"Get back here," Stuart yelled. His lungs burned; he breathed poison.

The slithering snake queen stopped and focused on Baruna, with a basilisk glare. Her eyes glittered a putrid yellow, and her black mouth opened, releasing sickly green vapors.

The Sikh woman, strong as she was, fell to one knee under that baleful gaze. And yet she remained steady, firing off a shot from her laser pistol.

Her aim was true, and the beam hit the Queen of Disease just below her neck. If it hurt her, however, she did not show it. Instead, she advanced on the nearly prone woman who dared defy her.

Stuart had to rip off his helmet, and he fell to the ground. He had not eaten much and could not vomit, but his body was wracked by dry heaves.

Harper was beside him and she held her head in her hands as though the world was spinning around her.

Focusing as hard as he possibly could, Stuart fought to speak. "Save her, please!" he yelled hoarsely. His body slumped to the bloody ground, one body amongst many, but he was not yet covered by darkness. "Ghosts of Graben!" he boomed as best he could. "Reveal thyself."

Ajatar stopped suddenly. Her snake head whipped down, searching for whatever had stopped her. She hissed as *they* shifted into the visible spectrum.

As Stuart had hoped since the centipede man had fallen, the golems of Graben had joined them.

***

They tore her apart. Her powers were lethal to organic life, but the automatons had no fear of disease, of pestilence, of illness. Ajatar remained powerful, but for all her strength she was outnumbered and outmatched. Her body was cut and torn in many places before she shrieked and slid away.

Head ringing, Stuart climbed to his feet. Harper had gained her footing first and together they supported each other as they unsteadily weaved toward Baruna. She was alive, though blood leaked from her eyes, streaming down her face, and bunching as it gathered at her neck.

The golems did not give chase to the snake queen. They gathered expectantly, a few hundred of them.

At that moment, a ball of flame shot forth, and landed amongst the golems. The three humans had to turn away, so bright was the light, so hot was the flame. When they turned back, half of the golems were gone; no doubt invisible. The other were so much melting slag.

The aspect of Ra, known as Mind, manifested before them. Though dressed in the same robes, he had changed. It had changed. The falcon head was mostly taken up by one large cyclopean eye, and he was carrying a twisted staff made of braided obsidian. Behind him were three desert ghouls and two centipede men.

A shout announced the arrival of Acan and Erinle and half a dozen others were beside them. Most of the invading monsters had fallen or fled. Most of the defending denizens of Selvage were wounded or dead.

Stuart was beginning to suspect just how they had been used by Acan, but there was no time for confrontation. Still woozy from the pestilence, still weak-kneed from the prospect of battle, Stuart nonetheless charged forward with the others.

Lasers blasted, talons tore, monsters roared, and men died. Above it all, the glowing aspect of Ra known as Mind swelled with power. His staff did not fire again; it did not need to. He fought with an aura as resplendent as Ajatar had been hideous and ghastly. The urge to prostrate himself, to surrender utterly to this shining god filled Stuart.

Laughter, a mocking harsh sound, broke through the soothing divine charm like ice cold water. It was a woman, but beneath the armor, Stuart was not sure which. She stood before the one-eyed aspect of Ra, with brazen confidence, though he stood at half her height.

"You fool. You've ruled for too long, and now you dance to my tune. The disc is mine. Ninkasi shall rule the gods on their long-awaited homecoming."

The Mind of Ra looked as much confused as it was irritated, but it dutifully lowered the staff and pointed it at the group of them.

"*YOU SHALL DIE,*" it said, in a voice that though a shadow of Ra, was nonetheless puissant, fearsome.

"I think not, Sun God. Your time has passed."

Acan appeared beside Harper and whispered something. She clapped her hands once, very precisely.

Darkness fell.

It wasn't the full calignosity of midnight, but it was instantly hard to see. Stuart could only see Mind because he glowed, but the aspect of Ra instantly faded. He shrank, too, until his dim, small body tumbled to the ground.

Even with the fall of their god, the ghouls and centipede men charged forward. Stuart did not even have a chance to feel fear before they were caught by an invisible wall. *The golems are still here*, Stuart realized. *Some of them, anyway.*

The battle was over. Or nearly so. Ninkasi took off her helmet, and Acan joined her. They strode to the fallen Falcon Lord and leaned over. Stuart could not see in the dim light exactly what happened. But when they stood again, they held in their hands a faintly gleaming disc as big as a shield.

"We have the eye of Ra!" Ninkasi shouted triumphantly. The surviving citizens of Selvage, of whom there about twenty, cheered. It seemed a paltry prize for the death of so many. Ninkasi strode back up the hill and most of the people of Selvage joined her.

Acan, however, walked gingerly across the battlefield to join the three humans. "You can take off your helmets now," he said. All three of them did so. He cupped his hands, and they each drank deeply from it.

Their injuries healed, their cuts closed, their heads stopped throbbing; they glowed with soft energy as they healed.

"You have my thanks," Acan said. "You brought the darkness from Graben. You brought the one thing that could fell the Falcon Lord."

"We didn't do anything," Harper said.

Stuart collected his journal and backpack as they spoke.

"You did what was needed of you," Acan said. "And it will not be forgotten."

"Can we go home now? You have the disc of Ra. I didn't realize it was actually his eye," Harper said.

Acan laughed. "Of course. Otherwise we could just borrow it." His face became more serious. "You must be exhausted, but there are ceremonies to be followed, graves to be dug, procedures that must precede, that sort of thing. Come back to Selvage, and we will discuss it further."

"I don't suppose we have any choice," Harper said.

"Not really, no," Acan agreed, his voice merry again.

It was a long journey back to Selvage.

Chapter 29

It was not as beautiful as the Cinnamon Hills, it was not as awe-inspiring as the ghost city of Graben, and it certainly was not as imposing as hulking Omphalos. Selvage possessed a dignified, pastoral charm all its own, however. They reached it by long riding, first through the Hills for what felt like days. They then rode up into the mountains, across passes of ice and snow, between rocky peaks draped in frosted mantles. They followed a glacial blue-grey trickle as it tumbled out of the mountains and expanded into a river. Eventually, the rocky harsh terrain and scattered pines gave way to fields of white flowers and maple trees hidden in a valley.

The enormous green building, that verdant monolith, was evident even from the mountains, but the low tree-homes of Selvage only grew visible just as the air warmed once more. Acan and three others rode on moose. They had many rider-less animals with them, with bodies of the fallen slung across of them. Ninkasi had stayed with the other survivors and all the crystal armor and heliacal contraptions to use the sunlit area for recharging.

Not many stayed. Most of the Selvagians who had set forth to battle were dead. Stuart had been surprised at how sad he was to learn that Erinle had not survived the battle. He had also found Nakka's dead body amongst the bulk of spider corpses. She had not been close to him, but he found himself growing despondent and reserved on the long ride back. Almost no one talked the entire time.

Those who had stayed behind in Selvage greeted them. Word had reached them already somehow, and none seemed to be very sad. The three humans watched as the gods reunited. The eye of Ra was passed to a short, slender gnomish looking god with a long beard.

The Upworlders strode across the green grass to Acan. His smile faded as he beheld them.

"We want to go home," Stuart said.

Some of the other gods, who had watched them approach, discretely disappeared. Stuart felt something bad was coming.

"We can't actually do that," Acan said. "I'm afraid there's been a change of plan."

"Dammit!' Stuart roared. "I knew it."

"We had a deal," Harper said. "You suggested it. Right after we rescued you."

"I do apologize. I suppose from your perspective it must look like we used you. But you have to think of it from our perspective."

"What perspective is that?" Harper half-yelled.

"We are gods. You are humans," Acan said simply.

"Human we may be, but we are not tools to be used!" Stuart said.

Acan laughed. "That's exactly what you are. That is why you were made. Listen, we have not had the use of the disc since we left Omphalos. Our needs are greater than yours."

"Because you're gods?" Stuart questioned.

"That too. Also because there are a thousand of us and three of you."

"There were four," Baruna said. "Five when we left the boat. And there are many more waiting on the boat for us as well. They are depending on us."

"Why can't you use the disc to send us home and then use it for your own?" Harper asked.

Stuart nodded at the sagacity of the question.

"The disc contains much of the Falcon Lord's power. But it is not infinite. We will use half of it to bring our fallen back to life."

"They will come back?" Stuart asked.

"Of course. We are gods. Immortality is an inherent aspect of that."

"Does that mean?" Baruna began to ask, though she trailed off.

"Your man? Sorry, it doesn't work like that. Mortality and all."

Acan lowered his voice and held out his hand in appeasement.

"Others disagree, but I want to invite you to stay here. With us. You can become honorary citizens of Selvage. You brought the golems, after all; you brought the darkness. We owe our victory to you."

"Turds! My *jaanu* died for the mission," Baruna said hotly.

"As did Maxwell," Harper added. This wasn't strictly true, but no one called her on it.

"Yes. We cannot just give up," Baruna said. "Is there not a way back without the disc?"

"Not for mortals," Acan said. "I am sorry, truly, but the sooner you accept your life here, the happier you will be."

"Tell us about the golems," Stuart said. "That is why you sent us to Graben, isn't it?"

Acan could not hide the look of surprise. "Clever," he said. Behind him, the bodies had mostly been unloaded, and the megamoose led back to their pastures. The gods that had been overtly *not* listening were now dispersing back into the spread out city. "I have an issue I must address. Find me later and I will tell you all I know."

***

"Have you ever been to Graben?" Stuart asked. They had bathed and changed into clean clothing. Sleeping on the firm ground, rather than an ambling moose, had been nice enough that they had slept for some time. Hungry bellies woke them, and now the three humans had found Acan in a dining hall. Before them were crispy baked mushrooms, a spicy mushroom soup, and a dark chewy jerky gathered on a long red-and-white table that grew from the earth.

"No. The guardians would not allow a god to enter."

"Ra entered," Harper pointed out.

"The Falcon Lord does as he pleases." Acan finished a bowl of soup and grabbed another. He dipped the mushroom jerky into it, letting it soften from the spicy broth.

"It was men, wasn't it?" Stuart asked. "That's the only thing that makes sense. Men started the city somehow. The golems only serve men."

"A bit simplified, but you are not wrong," Acan said.

"How was there ever a human city here, below the mantle?" Harper asked.

"And how could they defy gods?" Stuart added.

"That is a long story," Acan said.

"We have time," Baruna said. She was not eating; her arms were crossed and her body was angled away from Acan, who was beside her and across from Stuart and Harper.

Acan sighed. "When I said I'd tell you everything, I didn't mean all of history. Very well. When we left the surface, we brought many humans with us. Some we enhanced with magic, with knowledge, with machinery, with breeding. They became, by your standards, super-humans. Demigods. Some few went back to the surface and achieved fame."

"Like who?" Stuart asked.

Acan frowned at the interruption. "Heracles. Sigurd. Ghengis Khan. Jimmy Page. That's not important. Most stayed here and quietly stewed in their roles as servants. Some were not happy, however. The super-humans led a rebellion of regular humans. This was when most of us remained in Omphalos."

"Good," Baruna said.

"It happens that I agree with you. Many of my compatriots expect worship and obeisance without any effort on their parts. It is no wonder the humans, many of whom were nearly as powerful as someone like me, wanted more. They left, messily I might add, and founded Graben."

"Didn't you go after them? It doesn't seem like the kind of thing Ra would just allow?" Stuart asked.

"Had the Falcon Lord led an army just then, the result would have been inevitable. The humans would have been captured without much effort. However, something else happened. Sky Father, the once partner of Ninkasi, led many of us to freedom from Omphalos just after that. We were the, you might say, progressive gods. We tired of the cruelty and the nonstop worship."

"Good for you," Harper said.

"Your approval means everything," Acan replied with mock dignity. "At first we settled in the area of the battle, beneath the true light, but we were driven from there. Sky Father was captured and many fell. This valley was discovered, and we have since endeavored to live here as peacefully as possible."

"And the humans?" Baruna asked. Her recently constant surliness was just perceptibly tinged with interest.

"Yes. After driving us here, the gods of Omphalos gathered an army. But they found a marble city—a living wonder—it blocked magic. The golems the humans had created to serve them were immune to the charms and curses of the gods. The plagues too. It was then that the Falcon Lord split himself, then that the Seven Staffs of Sunrise were created. These were powerful weapons as you know. But it cost too much to break through. This was not the beginning of monster breeding and fighting in Omphalos, but it served to amplify it to a prodigious degree."

"The monsters were bred to fight Graben?" Stuart asked.

"To a large extent, yes."

"So Graben was left unmolested. What happened to the humans? Why was it empty when we found it?"

Acan sighed. "I don't know. The most popular guess is that they abandoned their city and returned to the surface, where they and their descendants yet rule from the shadows. Probably some of them did. I suspect certain elements in Omphalos found stealth could succeed where martial might did not. I suspect most of the super-humans of Graben were murdered. It is certain that many golems were captured and turned into servants. Some were studied and turned into the warriors that you encountered your first time here."

"That's horrible," Harper said.

"History is horrible," Acan said. "For your kind and mine. It remains better than the alternative."

"Which is?" she asked. Her meal was half-eaten before her, but she was too caught up to finish it now.

"Extinction."

"And the darkness?" Baruna asked, before that word had a chance to get too heavy. "How did they create that?"

"They didn't strictly create it. It was always here. We live in darkness with an illusion of light." He sounded bitterer than Stuart could recall ever hearing. "Some of the more powerful golems were so strongly imbued with anti-magic that they could dispel our façade of illumination."

"Smart," Harper said. "That was developed as a counter to the sun god?"

"Actually, at first," Acan said. "I believe it was just because humans, like all diurnal animals, preferred to sleep in the dark. Their effectiveness against the Falcon Lord was fortunate indeed."

"So, in essence, you have man-made machines dispelling the illusions of gods?" Stuart asked.

"That's a nice metaphor." Acan seemed to scowl for a moment, but if so, it was gone as quickly as it appeared.

"After the battle we fought, where did the golems go?" Harper asked.

"Most did not survive. They were designed to protect humans, after all. The fulfilled their function."

"Why didn't they turn it to darkness when Ra stormed into the city?" Baruna asked. Her voice was deceptively calm.

"As I understand it, The Falcon Lord entered the city in a different form. That of Amun-Ra. This *incarnation* would not have the same limitations. It's also possible the golems needed to be given instructions. I doubt any of you would have thought to give them."

"By that same logic," Stuart asked. "What triggered the golems in this battle? How did they know?"

"He told me to clap," Harper said. "It was as simple as turning on a light switch."

Acan finished lifted the bowl to his lips and slurped down the rest of his soup.

"Now, I hope I answered your questions. I am needed elsewhere, but I will find you later, and help you into your homes. I seem to recall you prefer returning to the same place every night rather than different ones?"

"We do," Harper said.

"Strange, but then I suppose instinct is strong in animals," Acan mused.

* * *

Acan left them, and the humans gathered together conspiratorially. Of course, the gods could listen to them if they desired; this they all knew. Each hoped that they remained beneath their notice.

"He's lying," Harper said. "I'm sure of it. Why would Ra change forms just to capture us, if it was a step, he wouldn't take to crush his enemies?"

"Good question. He sounded so bitter talking about the darkness too," Stuart said. "I tried to push him a little bit, and I think he showed a little of his true emotion."

"What if they want to return to the surface?" Baruna said. "What if they crave true sunlight that much?"

They all thought about that for a few moments.

"It explains why they don't have enough energy to send us back," Stuart said. It made so much sense that his mind was spinning.

"Wait. Was Ra trying to prevent it?" Harper asked, her voice lowered in awe. "Is that what the split of Selvage from Omphalos was in the first place?"

"We can guess all day," Stuart said. "Even if he's telling the truth, though, we owe it ourselves to get out of here."

"And go where?" Harper asked.

"Home," Stuart said.

"Sure," Harper said. "But how?"

It was then that a golem with a green Mohawk shifted into the visible spectrum before them.

Chapter 30

It happened like this: Before any of them could say anything, Baruna clapped her hands together. A deep darkness slumped across the city, and surprised exclamations of the gods rang out. It was just light enough to see vague shadows. Together the three of them carefully followed the golem out of the building and onto the grass.

Moving with unerring precision, the golem weaved them throughout Selvage. They did not encounter another being. At last, their Mohawked guide stopped before a building and motioned for them to enter.

With a helpless look at the others, Stuart stepped in.

Something softly glowed in the center of the room. He walked to it slowly, step by careful step. He knew what it was, of course. Instinctively, he understood exactly what lay there before him.

Stuart slung off his backpack, unzipped it, and stuffed the eye of Ra into it. The eye was too big to fit entirely, and he could not zip it back up again. It felt as though it might fall out, so he put it back on his front. On his way out, he saw some familiar vials, and threw those into the front pocket of his pack.

"What's up?" Harper asked.

"I've got the eye," Stuart said. "We need to go."

"How? Where? They can chase us down," Baruna said.

"We can get away," Stuart said.

"They're gods! I'm sure they can fly, or run faster than the wind. Where can we go?" Harper asked. "How can we get away?"

"There's only one option," Stuart replied. "We go the pasture. And we ride the megamoose away from here as fast as we can."

"Well, it's as good an idea as I can think of," Harper said.

"It's better," he answered. Turning to the golem, he asked, "Do you know where the portal to the moose field is?"

It seemed to understand him instantly, and it set off on another circuitous route. There were various lit up areas and bands of Selvagians wandering the village, but again they encountered no one.

The golem led them to another of the houses. The three went in and were greeted by a shimmering portal. It was wide and large enough to walk two megamoose at a time through, and the three of them easily fit. The golem did not follow them, or if it did so, remained invisible. They waved goodbye and stepped through.

The pasture was far enough away from Selvage that it was free of the darkness.

"What's that?" Harper asked.

Rushed though they were, Stuart was transfixed by the sight she had indicated.

A bubble shimmered with translucent luminosity. Behind that sheer curtain, massive, unkempt beasts tramped and tromped in the fields. One trumpeted a warning at them, trunk lifted high into the air.

"Mammoths!" Harper cried. "*Mammuthus primigenius.* I never thought to see them in real life."

"Can we ride them?" Stuart asked.

"I wouldn't want to try," Harper said. "They are territorial and could easily kill us just for entering their domain."

"Isn't it too hot for them? I mean, I couldn't keep my jacket on," Stuart asked.

Harper shrugged. "I don't know. Maybe the gods use magic to cool   them   off."
"We have to go," Baruna said. "They will be on our heels anytime now."

Harper reluctantly agreed. After riding for so long from the Cinnamon Hills, it was easy to quickly mount the megamoose, and ride away. A quick conversation resulted in a decision to ride back to where they had first entered the land; the long staircase and stone Moai.

Stuart kept looking back, but there was nothing behind them. It seemed they had not been discovered yet. They stopped once to let the moose drink from a stream. With their massive antlers, it took a deep and wide source of water for them to lower their heads. As they were doing so, Baruna removed her pistol, and shot at something behind them. She shot several times, her face wrapped in a frown.

"What the hell?" Stuart asked.

"They found us," Harper said.

"Relax," Baruna said. "It's only that plant that almost ate Keshav."

Stuart stared. It *was* where the plant had attacked them. It seemed so long ago now. Baruna's revenge seemed petty, but there was little they could do; the cobra lily was a steaming pile of compost.

Some time later, they were passed by a dozen terror birds. Fast as the moose could go, the birds were much, much faster. Either wary of the moose or used to seeing gods seated upon them, the birds did not bother them. Stuart thought about shooting one, but he did not want to risk angering the others.

Soon after that, however, Stuart glanced back and saw, not far away, at least ten gods behind them. They were mounted on mammoths; riding quickly and catching up.

"Ride!" Stuart called. They pressed their moose to dangerous speeds over the uneven ground. And yet their pursuers closed the gap by half. The mammoths could achieve speeds that no moose could match.

"Almost there," Harper called.

Ahead of them saw the first of the large statues. Their moose slowed, fighting the commands of their riders.

The human riders rode toward the circle of statues, but there was no sign of the staircase.

"No time!" Harper yelled. She leapt down from her beast into the tall grass.

Stuart followed her, gingerly holding his backpack with both hands.

Baruna remained on her moose; her hand was on her gun, and her eyes on their pursuers. They were close enough now that Acan was recognizable. He rode on the lead mammoth and did not look happy.

"What do I do with it?" Stuart asked.

"Throw it down. I don't know."

He set it down instead, smoothing some of the small grass just beneath one of the larger Moai. The rumble of mammoths grew louder, and Stuart could smell their powerful bestial scent

"Open Sesame," Stuart yelled, thinking of the *Pantheon.*

A black door opened in the air before them. It was opaque, completely black, and yet he could feel coldness seeping through. He hoped that the magic worked.

"Go," he said, shuttling Harper through before she could complain.

"You fools!" Acan was within earshot now. "You don't know what you're doing!"

"Baruna, go!" Stuart said.

She leapt from her moose and stood before the portal. Behind her, the gods surrounded them in a ring of mammoths. Acan leapt lightly from the back of his wooly beast.

"We can't leave it behind," Baruna said.

"We have to," Stuart said.

"Are you crazy? They can just come right after us."

"We have no choice!"

"We can fight," she said.

Stuart grabbed the pistol from her and shoved her through the portal.

Acan strode toward him. "You figured out our plans. Clever. But you can't stop us from hunting you down. And put down that pistol. It cannot hurt me."

Stuart raised his arm and shot the statue. He held the trigger, slicing through the stone at an angle. It took only a moment, and the top half of the stone was falling toward Stuart..

"No!" Acan cried, leaping for him. His mammoth roared with resounding force.

Stuart took a single step forward and imagined the portal closing as the giant stone fell upon the eye of Ra.

***

The cold smacked them with dynamic force. They had each grown accustomed to the sultry, oppressive temperatures below the earth. It was not snowing, and the sun shone in a brilliant blue sky, but the ice beneath their feet and the howling wind left no doubt about the world they had entered.

Stuart had to blink a few times, just to ensure this wasn't a dream or a hallucination. His shivering body left no doubt as to the reality of the situation, however. The glare of the sun on ice made him wish for sunglasses, an item he hadn't remembered existing since they'd descended down to the center of the Earth.

"We made it," Stuart yelled. His adrenalin was still up from the narrow escape.

"What did you do?" Baruna asked. He explained to her what had happened.

"Clever," Harper said. "Once again. Though I doubt it will keep them out forever."

"Ra has another eye, for one thing," Baruna said.

"Look at that," Harper said, pointing to their left.

Resting not more than twenty meters, was the Pantheon. It sat high on the ice, just as they had left it. But between them and the ship was something even more engaging.

"Look! I found penguins!" Stuart said. The little waddling creatures were surprised by the instantaneous emergence of the three humans, and they waddled away with croaks and squawks of dismay.

"I'm not trying to be funny," Baruna said. "But I could really use a hug right now." They joined her in a brief but heartfelt hug.

They were home.

Epilogue

Of all the bizarre things that happened to me since we left the Pantheon, I discovered the strangest one of all upon our return.

We spent weeks or months trapped beneath the mantle. Maybe longer, though in that largely nightless place, no one could know for sure. Subjectively, it felt like years. When I dreamed of coming back, I worried that my family would have declared me dead, my sister married, my brother too good at video games for me to ever play him again. Never once did I suspect the truth.

Above the surface, we were gone for less than a day. We found the ship much as we had left it. It was not easy to explain our strange clothes, our tan skin, the death of the other two men who set out. But none of us dared to whisper the truth. We had to settle for evasions, half-truths, and outright lies. Everyone was too relieved to press us too much. Apparently a massive storm swept in last night, and they were sure we were dead.

Captain Kugeon was coughing dark blood when we found him. I smuggled balche out from Selvage, and though it wasn't easy to get him to swallow it, eventually he did. He started to glow and healed before our eyes. It was miraculous. (Truly so, if I think about that word.) There was some left over, and Baruna took the rest to the other wounded passengers. It took all the balche we had, except for the bit around Baruna's neck, but I think we healed pretty much everyone.

I spoke to Baruna and Harper last night, when we finally had some time to ourselves. We are going to stick together for a while. Neither Harper nor I want Baruna to be alone right now, and she said she intended to visit her family in India. We were invited to accompany her. As to where Harper and I stand … shit, I don't know. That kiss in Graben feels like a long time ago. Another world ago. I think I'm comfortable being friends with her. At any rate, she has taught me a thing or two about how to live. We will see.

If you detect optimism and forward planning in this writing, you are correct. Thirty minutes ago (how nice it is to have time again!) I was awoken by the sound of a helicopter outside. We have been found, and some of the children on the ship have already been flown back to land. There are ice-breakers and rescue helicopters coming. They have been looking for us for two days, but in the fog it was impossible to find us, especially as they didn't know we had changed course. Tonight, we will be on land back in Ushuaia with restaurants, Wi-Fi, and all the comforts of civilization.

Things that I missed. Peanut butter on toast. (Keshav was right about North Americans and peanut butter.) A hot cup of coffee. A hot shower, for that matter. A small device that plays hundreds of songs right into my ears. I have to play some Cornershop in honor of Keshav as soon as I can. Relaxing without worrying about monsters eating me or angry gods.

This morning the three of us slipped back down onto the ice after we raided the cupboard of seven king size Cabury bars. It didn't take long to find a crack in the ice, where the turbulent sea peeked through at us. Harper unwrapped and threw all of them in. We watched as they sank into the sea. Will they make their way to Ek Chuaj? Or be eaten by an unwary octopus? I don't know, but I like to think that those Roasted Almond and Dairy Milk bars will somehow find their way to the bottom of the ocean, and be discovered by the denizens who live beneath the mantle.

And in the meantime? I still have my memory card. I just may have a story to tell . . .

THE END

To begin with, I would like to thank Gary Lucas, Dane T. Hatchell and the others at Severed Press for their hard work. This book would not exist in shape without them. Additionally, what you have just read would be significantly worse without the help of the redoubtable Garrett Calcaterra, eagle-eyed Rachel Hadfield, and Ashley "Don't You Even Know What SpellCheck Is?" Johnson. Thanks too to Wind Lothamer for initial discussions and to Oreon Lothamer, for agreeing to read it even though it wasn't Highlander fanfiction.

Much gratitude to my brother Jesse, who read a bit before finding a much more interesting video game and my sister Janessa, whom I still hope to convince to read Lord of the Rings someday. Above all, thanks to my mother, Cilicia Philemon, who encouraged my love of reading and is as supportive as possible, even though my books are too dark and violent for her to actually read.

Inspiration came from the BBC program Walking With Beasts and the board game Carcassone: Hunters and Gatherers. I recommend both to anyone with a further interest in megafauna.

Ahimsa Kerp
March 2015

www.ingramcontent.com/pod-product-compliance
Lightning Source LLC
Chambersburg PA
CBHW051946170626
46808CB00007B/2512